The Lilith Summer

Bring to a Boil and Separate
(*A Margaret K. McElderry Book*)

Moon & Me
(*A Margaret K. McElderry Book*)

I-163

F
Irw   Irwin, Hadley
           What about Grandma?

DATE DUE			
DEC 11			
APR 6			

MEDIALOG
Alexandria, Ky 41001

What About Grandma?

What About Grandma?

Hadley Irwin

A MARGARET K. MCELDERRY BOOK

Atheneum 1982 New York

LIBRARY OF CONGRESS CATALOGING IN PUBLICATION DATA

Irwin, Hadley.
  What about grandma?

  "A Margaret K. McElderry book."
  Summary: Caught between her grandmother's fierce
independence and her mother's solution of a nursing home,
Rhys grows up during a summer while experiencing her
first love.
  [1. Family life—Fiction. 2. Old age—Fiction.
3. Love—Fiction] I. Title.
PZ7.I712Wh   [Fic]   81–10809
ISBN 0–689–50224–9   AACR2

Published simultaneously in Canada by McClelland & Stewart, Ltd.
Composition by American–Stratford Graphic Services, Inc.
Brattleboro, Vermont
Manufactured by Fairfield Graphics,
Fairfield, Pennsylvania
Designed by Felicia Bond

FIRST EDITION

To
Paula

Contents

What About Grandma?

1

Grandmother's House

"Over the river and through the woods. To Grandmother's house we go," I sang in my best first-grade voice.

Mom didn't comment.

"Well, if this were November instead of June, and we were in a sleigh, it would sound better," I went on in my real voice.

Mom kept her eyes focused on the highway. "Rhys Ann, please do me a favor. For a while, just a little while, don't be sixteen. Any other age you want, but not sixteen."

"Okay. At least there'll be a lake. That motel last night didn't even have a pool."

"Yes. We can swim off your grandmother's dock."

"Anyway, there'll be something to do for a month."

"A month should be long enough. We can sort out her things. Arrange for the auction. I'll call the real estate dealer tomorrow and list the house."

"Boring." I shifted in the seat. We'd been driving steadily since stopping for lunch.

"Breaking up a household isn't particularly exciting." Mom glanced at the speedometer and eased up on the accelerator.

"Sounds like we're moving in with a demolition crew."

"That might be easier."

"How much farther?"

"Ten miles or so," she answered, switching on the radio.

My memory of Grandma's house was blurred. Only two things were distinct: the big glass front door, flanked by stained glass panels that made a rainbow on the hallway floor even on dark days, and the long winding staircase, sweeping up from the carved newel post.

"Will Uncle Dave be there?"

"No. He's coming for the sale. He said if we see anything in the house we want, we're to tape our names on the back."

"How much stuff is there?" I shifted again in the seat.

"A house full. Five bedrooms, sun porch, front parlor, sleeping porch, back parlor, dining room, kitchen, attic, basement. And your grandmother never threw anything away."

I hadn't been to my grandma's house since I was eight, which for me was half a lifetime ago. Mom, of course, went every summer in between her regular school year and her summer classes. But when I was nine, I began spending that time with my father and his family.

Mom and Dad were divorced when I was a baby, and though she had told me about him and I had pictures of him and he'd sent me presents on my birthday and Christmas, I hadn't actually seen him. Since I'd never known him, I hadn't particularly missed him. He was more like an uncle than a father. But the summer I was nine, he wrote to Mom and asked if I could come and stay for a couple of weeks, if she agreed and if I wanted to. Mom and I talked it over. I mean she didn't hate him or anything; in fact, she'd never said anything bad about him. It was just that they didn't want to live with each other.

At first I didn't especially want to go, but I didn't want to go with Mom to Grandma's either. After all, I'd been there almost every summer of my life. Besides, I thought it was important to see the other half of who I was. I know that doesn't sound like a nine-year-old, but in some ways I was more grown up than most kids, except for Kim, my best friend, probably because Mom and I had to take care of each other.

It was really lucky that my father and I liked each other. I decided he was a better father the way it was than if we'd lived together. His wife and kids were okay too. They weren't my family, but they were nice and didn't make me feel like an outsider. I was always happy to get home, though.

Right now, I wished I were home instead of being twisted like a pretzel and packed off to Grandma's house. I glanced at Mom. I knew she was tired.

"Mom, with all the stuff we have to do, how are you going to have any time to finish your work?"

"I'll have to make time. But we'll have two months free when we get back home the end of June."

I knew she was supposed to have those last chapters of her dissertation done by the end of summer.

"I'm never going to get a Ph.D. It's too much work.

I'd rather play golf. Wonder if the Preston course is any good?"

Golf was important to me. I took it very seriously, and if I kept on improving, it could mean a four-year college scholarship.

"Wish Kim could have come along."

Mom didn't answer.

I knew she didn't want to talk any more. She was never rude, but she could turn herself off. Even if she were sitting right beside you, she could sort of disappear.

For forty-two, she was quite good looking: short shiny hair, dark blue eyes, nice teeth—the kind they have in toothpaste ads—and skin as smooth and unwrinkled as mine. One thing about her, though, her face never changed very much, no matter what she was feeling. She seldom frowned and she didn't laugh often. If she thought something funny, there was this little twitch in the muscles at the corners of her mouth as if she'd like to laugh, but didn't quite know how.

I'd read a lot about how lonely it was to be an only child or how awful not to have a father in the home, but I didn't feel deprived. Mom and I were a family. I liked my mother. I really did. Of course she had her off moments when she refused to listen to reason, but on a scale of A to F, I'd give her a strong B-plus. Maybe even an A-minus.

Mom zoomed the car past a long semi and slipped back into the proper lane.

"How come we're taking care of grandmother's house? Why not Uncle Dave?"

"He's busy. He has a court case coming up."

"But he's her son."

6

"I'm her daughter. That makes all the difference."

It was a difference I did not understand. I couldn't figure it out. For example, there was no difference between Kim and me, except he was a boy, and I wasn't. He had to do the same stuff around his house as I did in ours. He always won when we played tennis, and I always won when we played golf.

Or maybe there was a difference. We were in a lot of the same classes in school, and the teachers always expected me to have the correct answer right away. They gave Kim plenty of time to think. On the other hand, whenever there was a disturbance in the classroom, Kim always got blamed even if Sheryl started it, and she usually did.

Funny, but I knew I wouldn't miss any of the gang I fooled around with. When I got back they'd be doing the same things they always did: riding around town in Sheryl's car, hanging out at the swimming pool, or hitting the drive-in theater twice a week. Kim was the only one who was interesting, and he might as well have been my brother. I felt as though I'd outgrown the rest of them.

What I'd really wanted to do that summer was to get a job in Colorado at one of those big resorts. In fact, I'd given Mom every reason I could think of for doing it, except the real one. I'd talked about saving money for college, the advantages of travel, the opportunity for responsibility. I hadn't mentioned that I was getting bored with the kids I ran around with, except Kim, and that I wanted to meet someone new. I wanted, just once, to meet someone who hadn't known me all my life, someone who wouldn't see me as a girl, but as a woman, which I practically was.

But I hadn't been able to convince Mom, and so we were both going to Grandma's for a month.

A mile before we even saw a town, we passed a big red-and-white sign that said "Preston City Limits."

"They must expect the town to grow." For some reason I felt obligated to keep a conversation going, for Mom had grown more and more quiet the closer we came to Preston.

"The town hasn't grown since I left for college, and every time I come back I feel as if I haven't grown either." Mom flipped on her turn signal. "We'd better stop at a grocery store and pick up something for dinner."

We pulled into a parking lot in front of a building that looked like a garage and turned out to be Joe's Super Market.

"I'll stay in the car. And don't forget coffee, or you'll be mad in the morning." I knew I was just postponing the inevitable, but I figured if I didn't get out of the car, I wasn't really in Preston.

From my view of the parking lot, I decided everyone drove big shiny pick-up trucks with CB antennae sprouting from their roofs. I still couldn't see much of the town for all the trees—trees even on main street, which was all of two blocks long. Maybe it was just as well Kim hadn't come with us. Preston was so quiet and peaceful, he'd have died of boredom.

Kim and I had lived on the same block since we were little kids, and we'd always been best friends, maybe because we were exactly the same age. We still spent a lot of time together. Somehow that was more fun than the dating a lot of the other kids did.

Mom returned and set the bag of groceries in my lap,

which was the only empty spot in the car. "Just a few minutes and we'll be at the house."

I noticed she didn't say "home."

The lake was pretty, trees around the edges, sailboats tacking back and forth, and there was a swimming beach.

Grandma's house was big and white with an open front porch that wound around one side and across the back where it had been made into a sun porch with a sleeping porch above. Towering elms hid the second story. Our tires crunched over the white rock drive and, beyond, the back yard sloped down to the lake.

"Wasn't this an awfully big house for her to take care of?"

"Toward the end it was almost too much," Mom said slowly. "She was stubborn. She didn't want to give it up."

We carried the groceries and our overnight bags up to the front door and walked right in.

"How come it's not locked?" I asked.

"Your grandmother never locked a door in her life. I doubt if there ever *was* a key to this house. Go around and open the windows. It's musty in here."

Mom disappeared into the kitchen.

The sun hadn't set, so I didn't bother turning on lights. I moved through the shadowed rooms. The hallway went straight through the house to the back porch, and I remembered how I used to make it my racetrack when I was little, bursting in through the front door, down the hall, out the back door, across the porch, around the house and in again. And there was the stone fireplace where I had hung my stocking on long-ago Christmas Eves.

Wood paneling was everywhere, not the kind we had

at home but dark, old, heavy-looking panels that reached only halfway up the walls. The furniture was big and ugly, but at least there weren't any stiff white doilies stuck on or under everything as there were at Kim's grandmother's.

And there were no pictures, except one in the living room, an oil painting of the lake with a setting sun. Even in the half light it glowed red and gold. I didn't go upstairs. I felt as if I were prowling around some stranger's house.

I found Mom out on the back porch step, sitting, smoking and watching the sun set on the other side of the lake. I kept telling her how unhealthy smoking was and that she was probably killing me too, but she just nodded and did it anyway.

"Who painted the picture in the living room?" I sat down beside her.

"Your grandmother."

"I didn't know she could paint."

"That's the only one she ever did, as far as I know. Said she wanted to see if she could do it, and when she found out she could, she stopped."

"That's crazy."

"Mother has always been unusual, in many ways."

It sounded funny when Mom said "Mother." Usually it was "your grandmother."

"You know what I remember most about this house, Mom? We'd be in the kitchen and she used to tell me this story about a Welsh witch who stole girls from their mothers. Then she'd pick up a broom and dance around, singing in a cackly voice that scared me to death. I thought she really could turn herself into a witch and steal me from you."

10

"I know." Mother looked out across the lake. "She used to sing it to Dave and me too. Twtti Wyn Hec."

And Mom began to sing:

> The sprites of Glyn Mawddy
> Will wring my old neck
> If anyone discovers
> I'm Twtti Wyn Hec!

"That was it," I said, hugging my knees to my chest. "She'd laugh in this awful voice and I'd shiver. Then she'd laugh again in her own voice and hug me.

"You know what I remember most about her?" I stood up and leaned against the iron railing. "Her eyes. So black. I never dared lie to her. She told me once her eyes were so black they could see right through me. Even in the dark."

"They probably could." Mom half chuckled. "She was familiar with the dark . . . her own dark."

A cool breeze blew across the lake, rippling the water into jagged streaks.

"I always tried to be as different from her as I could. Maybe every daughter does that." Mom squashed out her cigarette. "Now I think I'm growing more like her every day."

"What's wrong with that?"

"I'm not sure." Mom stood up. "It's just that I'm beginning to think maybe I've spent forty-two years reacting to her instead of acting for myself. And I don't know why. Even this house . . ."

"Is that why you came out here for a cigarette? I mean, that's kind of silly, isn't it? You're an adult. And besides, Grandma isn't here any more."

"I know, Rhys. It's something I'll have to sort out. It all started a long time ago." She put her hand on my shoulder. "We'd better find something to eat and get to bed. Tomorrow's going to be a long, difficult day."

It was funny climbing Grandma's stairs to go to bed. In our house everything was on one level, but at Grandma's it was as if there were three houses piled one on top of the other.

I paused on the landing and turned to look down toward the front door.

"How did she fall?"

"I don't know. I've never been sure exactly what happened. Her friend Virene found her in the morning."

All the bedroom doors were closed.

"It looks like a hotel," I said, opening a door. "Which one was Grandma's?"

"Don't you remember? She used them all. She was a prowler. Dave and I never knew, in the morning, where we'd find her. Once, when we were little and Father was still alive, we found her sleeping down by the lakeshore, just a blanket and a pillow—on the grass."

"You know, Mom. It's too bad I never really got to know Grandma."

"I don't think I ever got to know her either. Maybe no one did."

I chose the sleeping porch for my room with its three walls of windows that let in sounds from the lake. Just before I dropped off to sleep, I wondered if I'd be able to recognize my grandma the next day among the women in Preston's nursing home.

2

B r e a k i n g   U p

"I think I'll call a realtor first," Mom said the next morning. Mom was efficient. She always planned her day. "Maybe he can recommend an auctioneer and we can get a date set up for the household sale."

"Won't Grandma want to keep anything for herself?"

I was beginning to feel funny poking into Grandma's house. I knew I wouldn't want anyone coming into my room and prowling through my things.

"Some clothes, maybe. She doesn't have much room out there." Mom had trouble saying "nursing home." "But Dave said that when he was here last week she was in good spirits, perfectly agreeable to our disposing of things. He said she's finally given up the idea of trying to come home. A broken hip is serious for someone her age. And you know she's always refused to move in with either Dave or us."

Mom sounded as if she were arguing with herself instead of talking to me.

"What do you want me to do?"

"Well, why don't we start making a list of everything in the house—the furniture, room by room. You could start upstairs in my old bedroom, there at the back. Then, after lunch, we'll get cleaned up and go out. Visiting hours don't begin until two."

Mom and I had agreed long ago that bedrooms were private places, so I almost felt like knocking on the door. I didn't know how other families worked, except for Dad's and I really wasn't a part of it, and I hadn't been a part of Grandma's since I was little. Mom and I, even though we loved each other and were together, somehow managed to live separately. We both liked it that way.

I didn't knock. I walked through the door and looked around. The room was not like Mom's at home; it looked as if it belonged to a girl, not a mother. It's hard to imagine your mother as a girl. There were high school yearbooks, a red felt school letter, and a hand-lettered sign: "Eve's Room: Contaminated Area."

Eve was my Mom's name. Once I asked why Grandma named her that and Mom said, "It amused her, somehow. Dave was eleven when I was born, so she called me Eve because I was the family's first woman." Kim thought the name was neat. He thought the same thing about my mother. He said he wanted to have someone like her as his first woman.

In the bedroom closet, in plastic bags, was an assortment of long, old-fashioned formals and pleated full skirts, all pastel-colored. I couldn't imagine Mom in any of them. I wondered if I would have liked her then.

A bird's-eye-maple bed, matching dresser, night stand, study desk—I made my list and moved to the other rooms.

* * *

"Wynnie said you'd be moving in today!"

A voice ran through the house like a trumpet call. "Can you use some help?"

"Virene!" I heard Mom call. "Rhys! Come down. It's a friend of your grandmother's."

I started down the stairs. A massive woman filled the front door, her wide smile glowed above a series of chins.

"Well, I'll be damned! She's grown to be the spitting image of her grandma. How are you, Rhys?"

The woman was a blaze of color; her graying hair, piled high, shone bluish in the light above thin black eyebrows, arched in surprise.

She grabbed me around the waist and put her other arm over Mom's shoulder. "Golly, I'm glad you're here. Wyn'll be tickled to death. Got the coffee pot on?"

She herded us to the kitchen, and while Mom and I sat at the table, she made the coffee and talked.

"It sure was a shame. I always thought it was partly my fault. I should have come in with her that night. You know what happened, don't you? You know where we'd been?"

Mom shook her head as if afraid to ask.

"Wyn didn't want me to tell you, but we'd been to the old-time dance at the Moose Lodge. Danced every dance, too. I did, anyway, and that's not bad for a sixty-eight-year-old. I didn't see Wyn sitting out any dances either. We got home a little late. I dropped her off. I wanted to come in with her, but you know Wyn. She puts her mind to something and you can't talk her out of it."

"She fell that night, then?"

"Sure she did. When I found her the next morning, she had on the same outfit she wore to the dance. Just imagine. Lying there all night with a broken hip. And would you believe, when I came in she looked up and laughed. You know what she said?"

"I have no idea," Mother said taking a cup of coffee from Virene.

"She said, 'That last two-step was worth it, Vi, even if it was with Harley Strum.' You remember Harley?"

I gathered from Mom's expression that Harley Strum wasn't one of Preston's leading citizens.

"We had ourselves a night, Wyn and me. She paid a pretty high price for it." Virene rummaged through the cupboard and set an ash tray in the middle of the table.

"Don't you smoke, Eve?"

"I don't know why, but not in Mother's house."

"Wyn wouldn't care. She doesn't say anything when I do. But let's move out to the back step."

And we did.

"You know, Eve, I asked her to come live with me. We get along well together." Virene let herself down on the step, hanging firmly to the iron grillwork.

"And she wouldn't hear of it." Mom made it a statement, not a question.

"Got real huffy when I suggested it. You know how she is. Said, 'Just because my hip's weak, doesn't mean my brain is.' You don't tell Wyn what to do."

"I know," Mom said quietly. "But now she doesn't have a choice."

"I'm surprised she gave in so easy, though. She's really going to let you sell this place?"

"Dave convinced her."

"Who're you listing it with?"

"Parker's."

16

"Good. I was married to one of them once. They're honest. I suppose you got Owens for an auctioneer?"

"Yes," Mom answered.

"One of my ex-daughters-in-law married him. He'll cry a good sale for you. Going to keep any of the stuff?" Mother sipped her coffee. "A few things, I suppose."

"Well, if you need any of it trucked back, I'll get Buell—out at my truck stop—to haul it for you . . . cheap."

Virene never did get around to helping us, but by the time she left, I knew that she owned not only a truck stop, which she said she got from her first husband, but also a beauty shop—"The AAA Beauty Salon. Named it so's it'd be the first item in the phone book."—a fast food cafe out on the highway, a garbage route, and "a farm or two down on the bottoms."

After Virene left, the real estate man came. He stood in the hallway and peered up into the stairwell.

"You realize, it may take some time to unload this place. Expensive to heat, I bet. Well kept, though, I must say."

I looked at Mom, but I couldn't tell what she was thinking.

He glanced into the front parlor. "Fireplace work?"

"I think so," Mom muttered.

"Location is excellent." He stood in the back porch doorway. "You could probably sell off a lot or two down there by the lake."

Mom followed behind him, her arms folded across her chest. I did not follow them through the upstairs or down to the basement. The appraiser was turning Grandma's house into a piece of property, and I didn't like it.

They finally came up from the basement and stood in the front hall.

"It's really a family house. Young families have trouble financing places like this. It needs remodeling and re-decorating. Modernizing. Why don't you let me get some figures together and I'll be in touch?"

"That will be fine," Mom said. She didn't come back to the kitchen right away. I finally went into the hall. She was still standing by the door, looking out across the front lawn.

"Do you think anyone will buy it?" I asked.

"I don't know."

"I hope nobody buys it."

"It's only a house, Rhys. Your grandmother always said a person should never become so attached to any-thing that she cannot give it up. But it's easier to give advice than follow it."

As we left for the nursing home, soon after, I saw Mom pause in the front hall and run her hand along the bannister, almost like a caress.

"Now we must remember to be natural," Mom said as she backed the car out of the drive. "Don't be sur-prised if your grandmother is in a wheelchair. She was when Dave was here last week. When I saw her last Christmas, right after the fall, she was terribly weak and uncertain. Not at all like herself. Almost as if she had shrunk."

"Do we have to stay long?"

"Oh, no. We won't want to tire her this first time."

"What'll I say to her?"

"Just visit. We won't mention what we've been doing. About the auction and all. There'll be time for that later. We'll pretend we're here for a little vacation."

18

"Honest?"

Mom gave me a sideways glance that told me I'd said the wrong word. I decided the rules for aging were different from the rules for living.

We followed a road that skirted the lakeshore.

"Is the nursing home on the lake too?"

"No." The corner of Mom's mouth tightened. "Lake frontage is expensive."

Sunset Haven was on the far side of town just before the farmland began. The "home" sprawled like an octopus with rows of matching windows. We parked in a section marked "Visitors Only," which I thought was kind of silly. Why else would anyone come to a nursing home except to visit?

Mom didn't get out of the car right away. She shut off the engine and drew in a deep breath. I sort of knew how she was feeling. That's the way I feel whenever I have to make an important putt. I know I have to do it, but I put it off as long as I can.

"There's something about seeing your own mother in a nursing home . . ." She sighed.

"It'll be okay, Mom," I assured her. "We can pretend she's just visiting."

Mom gave me another strange look. "What age are you being now? Twelve or twenty-one?"

We walked together into Sunset Haven.

Mom headed for the reception desk, and I stood just inside the front door, flanked by artificial palms. Beyond was a display case of potholders, crocheted doilies, embroidered pillow cases, and stuffed animals, with a sign: "For Sale by Sunset Haven."

"Where do I find Room two-twelve?" I heard Mom ask.

The halls were lined with old men and women in chairs, sitting as if they had not moved for hours. A television set droned from the far end of the room, but no one was watching, only gazing, like faces painted on a sideshow canvas.

"Hush. There, there," a thin voice whispered from behind the plastic palm. "It won't be much longer."

"But my children. They should be here."

"They will come. It will not be much longer. Shhhh."

I tried to look between the leaves, but they were too thick. I stepped forward to see who was talking. A tiny woman, her face criss-crossed with wrinkles, sat alone crooning to her hands that moved like restless spiders in her lap. She looked up. Her eyes were green blanks, half hidden under a fringe of silky gray hair.

I moved back into the doorway.

I turned away. Beyond the other palm, an expanse of window fronted on a lawn, the kind you look at, not walk on. As I moved toward the window, I came face to face with a woman sitting erect in a straight chair. Her green pantsuit and red blouse stood out like an exclamation point. With one hand she hugged a sturdy black purse; the other grasped a cane as if it were a scepter. Her hair, a soft white cloud, framed a face dominated by eyes —black and deep and shining.

"Grandma?" I began.

She looked me straight in the eye. "You're late."

It was Twtti Wyn Hec! I would have known her anywhere.

Beside my grandma's chair was a suitcase.

3

Going Home

"Mother!" Mom rushed over to us. "The nurse . . . she says you've signed yourself out!"

"That's right." Grandma sniffed. "I'm going home." She sat even straighter, her lips a firm line.

"But, Mother. You can't."

Grandma waved her cane. "My room's already taken. The woman's moving in this afternoon."

My usually self-contained mother flushed and stammered, "But Dave said . . . Dave said everything . . . was settled."

"David was wrong." Grandma looked out the window as if dismissing the whole matter.

"But the house . . . the sale . . . the auction . . ."

"There's not going to be a sale."

Mom looked at me, her eyes like a bewildered child's. Grandma stood up slowly, leaning heavily on the cane. "Now help me with my suitcase. I'm going home!"

"But, Mother. The steps. The stairs . . ." Mom's hand waved vaguely.

"What about them?"

Grandma threaded her purse on one arm and reached for her suitcase.

"Mother, don't be silly. You know very well what about the stairs. What are you going to do? Crawl? On your hands and knees?"

"If I have to, I will."

Mother turned to me, her face tight. "Rhys. Carry your grandmother's suitcase."

The ride home took place in silence, Mom staring straight ahead and Grandma looking out the side window.

Slumped in the back seat, I looked at my mother and my grandmother. Even from behind, you could tell they were mother and daughter. Although they were looking in different directions, there was something about the way they held their heads, something about the squareness of their shoulders that made the relationship unmistakable. They were sitting only a foot or two apart, yet there didn't seem to be any closeness between them. I couldn't imagine them touching each other. I knew then it was going to be a long four weeks.

Mother and I helped Grandma up the front steps.

"I can walk by myself, now," she said, shrugging us off. "I'm going out to my back porch to look at my lake. I want to hear the water. It laps differently, you know, from any other lake in the world.'

She walked carefully down the hallway.

"Mother," Mom said. "Dave said you were in a wheel chair just last week."

Grandma stopped. "I might have been. Everybody has to be somewhere. And as for Dave . . . he assumes too much . . . at least about me." And she disappeared into the porch.

We stood like two schoolgirls whispering outside the principal's office.

"Mom! She tricked us! She tricked us into coming out here for four weeks to take care of things when she didn't have any intention of selling the house or anything."

"Well, Rhys, you'll have to admit it worked. Didn't it?" Mom almost laughed. "She got her way."

"The realtor? The auctioneer!"

"I know. We'll have to talk to your grandmother about that."

"Now?" I asked.

"Now!" my mother said and marched down the hall.

I followed her to the porch. Grandma looked up from her easy chair and smiled sweetly at us. "My! Just smell that breeze. And those lilacs. Do you know what we got in the nursing home? The left-over flowers from funerals. In our rooms! Isn't that disgusting?"

I had to agree.

"Mother," Mom began in her usual efficient voice. "What are we going to do about the house? I've already had the realtor in and set a date with the auctioneer for the household sale."

"Cancel!" She tapped her cane on the floor—one tap.

"Rhys and I can only stay four weeks."

"Did I ask you to stay longer?"

"What will you do when we have to leave?"

"We'll see about that when the time comes. I can tell you what I'm *not* going to do. I'm *not* going back to the nursing home. I'm *not* going to live with you nor Dave, or anyone else. And I'm *not* going to be a burden. I'm going to stay here."

"Grandma—" I broke in.

"Don't 'grandma' me! Right now I don't feel like anyone's grandma . . . or anyone's mother, for that matter."

"Okay," I persisted. "But will you be all right by yourself?"

"There's always Virene. We have a system. First thing when I get up, I put my geranium in the front window. When Vi goes by in the morning, she looks for it. If it's not there, she knows something's wrong. That's why she was the one who found me when I fell."

Mom sat down on the ottoman in front of Grandma's chair. "Mother. Now be honest. You tricked us into coming out here. Do you think it was fair? Why didn't you just tell us? We'd have come . . . for four weeks."

"Because nobody asked *me*. You and David told me. You assume too much."

I stood in the doorway feeling like a spectator. This was a contest between two stubborn, strong-willed women and I wasn't sure whose side I was on, Mom's or Twtti Wyn Hec's.

"At least let us move your bed downstairs. Out here on the porch. Wouldn't you like that?"

"No! Leave things as they are."

Later that afternoon, while Grandma napped on the sofa, Mom phoned the realtor and the auctioneer to cancel the sale and placed a long-distance call to my uncle.

"What did he say?" I whispered as if we were conspirators.

24

"First he laughed. Then he said we should have known. When did either of us ever control Mother? He said not to worry. He'd call the nursing home and make sure there'd be a place for her when we leave. Let her have her way. Then we'll do what we have to do for her own good."

"It isn't quite fair, though. Is it? To Grandma?" I wanted to say it was sneaky.

"No. It's sad. But very necessary. We're doing it only because we love her."

I started out to the kitchen thinking about Mom's "because." I wondered what happened to grandmas who weren't loved. I turned back, went up to Mom and touched her arm. "You know, sometimes I think 'poor Grandma.' And sometimes I think 'poor you.'"

Mom squeezed my hand. "It's not always easy to be a daughter," she said, and went upstairs to her room.

After dinner, Grandma announced, "I'm tired now. I'm going to bed."

I offered to help. Mom shook her head. I sat on the porch and listened.

It took them ten minutes to get up the stairs.

When the struggle was over, Mom collapsed in the chair beside me.

"Rhys. Is there any coffee left? I could drink a whole pot tonight."

Mom's hair usually lay straight and flat, every strand in place, but now it stuck up at odd angles as if she had been out in a wind.

Grandma made it up the stairs that first night, but I think Mom, not Grandma, did the crawling.

4

Settling In

The next morning, early, the kitchen door burst open. Mom and I looked up from our bowls of cereal.

"Wynnie!"

It was Virene. She swooped down on Grandma. "I about died! I went out to the nursing home and they told me you'd checked out! For a minute I thought . . ."

"They're careless with language out there," Grandma muttered. "Finish your cereal, Rhys."

All in one large motion, without asking, Virene poured herself a cup of coffee, dragged a chair to the table and lit a cigarette.

I looked at my mother. Her mouth was slightly open.

"What's the matter with you, Wynnie? Why didn't you tell me? I'd have come and picked you up. And you're so right. The nursing home's no place for you."

"It's no place for anyone. People die there. Of boredom, mostly." Grandma wiped her mouth. "Vi, you don't know how well I slept last night in my own bed."

"How'd you manage the stairs?"

"Wasn't too much trouble. I took them slowly." Grandma flicked a toast crumb from the table cloth.

Mother's jaw tightened.

"I don't like it, Wyn. Those stairs started everything in the first place. I told Eve all about it yesterday. Now what say I move your bed down to the sun porch? What do you think?"

Grandma smiled angelically and folded her hands in her lap. "I think that's a splendid idea, Virene. It's always been my favorite room."

Mom and I offered to help Virene with the move, but she waved us off. "There's only room on those stairs for me and a mattress. I can do it myself."

She was right. By the time I had finished my cereal, Virene was carrying the last part of Grandma's bed out to the porch.

"How about another cup of coffee?" Virene settled herself at the table and smiled at Grandma. "Well, Wynnie. Now that's taken care of, what I came to see you about is that Buell and I are taking off up north in the van for a little walleye fishing. Figure on being gone about a week."

"Buell's Vi's fishing companion," Grandma explained. "He works for her at the truck stop."

Vi began to talk again and Mom stood up. "Virene, if you're going to be around for a few more minutes, I think I'll run Rhys out to the golf course. Maybe we can arrange for a locker and greens fees so she can play a little golf."

"A golfer, huh?"

"Sort of." I don't know why I felt apologetic.

"Silly game, chasing a ball around a pasture," Grandma said, gazing out toward the lake.

"To each his own, Wynnie. Fishing for me. Golfing for Rhys. That herb garden of yours for you. Do you know, Rhys, your grandmother claims she can cure anything with those herbs. Got to admit it did clear up my gout last winter, didn't it, Wyn?"

"That and putting you on a diet." Grandma chuckled again. The whole scene was like a play: Vi on center stage and Grandma providing the audience.

As I started for the door, Vi shouted, "Say, Rhys. If you get hungry or thirsty out there at the golf course, stop in at the pro shop. Tell them Vi sent you."

"Sure. Thanks," I called back without the slightest intention of ever using Vi's name.

When we got back from the golf course, Virene was gone and Grandma was standing down by the lake.

"Where's Vi?" Mom hurried across the lawn.

Grandma turned, the breeze ruffling her hair into white puffs. "She left a few minutes after you did."

"But what if you'd fallen again?"

"I'd probably have stayed there until you got back. Eve, I'm not your child. I'm a grown woman and you have to let me live my own life."

Mother didn't answer.

It didn't take long for the three of us to stake out our own territories: Grandma on the sun porch, Mom in her upstairs study, and I on the golf course. I played every morning. I didn't stop at the pro shop.

There was no open hostility in Grandma's house, just a constant friction. After all, Grandma was used to living alone and Mom and I certainly weren't used to living with her.

Grandma's habit of wandering around in the night had not changed, and I knew Mom was staying awake listening.

"I have a little trouble breathing at night," Grandma explained. "It must be the humidity."

It wasn't just Grandma. It was Mom too. Grandma was able to move in and out of the house with the use of her cane, but every time she started down the back step, Mom's breath caught. Even I couldn't stand the way she hovered over Grandma. At the same time, I felt sorry for Mom. It was as if she were trying to do everything just right, trying too hard. I wondered if that was what she'd been like when she was my age.

Every day was pretty much the same. I always knew what was going to happen next. I wondered if when you got older, you got stuck like a needle on a phonograph record, spinning around in the same circles.

Grandma's circle began when I got home from playing golf.

"It's twelve thirty, Rhys. Do you mind turning the radio to KCRI? Nine-twenty. It's time for Emma Sage and the local news."

The news *was* local, straight from the police blotter or the hospital or mortuary. Emma always mispronounced words. "Arnie Sheffield suffered a Cadillac arrest and passed away last night. Arrangements are pending. Mrs. Ethel Smith suffered a traffic accident last night and is now under seduction in the Memorial Hospital." I thought it was gross. Grandma always laughed.

As soon as Emma was off the air, it was the herb garden.

"Now, Rhys. I watered this morning, but it does need weeding. Shall we go out and get it done?" It was not a question. It was a command.

"Sure," I muttered and trudged ahead of her across the lawn down to the garden.

Mom had told me Grandma used to go to the woods every spring and bring back healing herbs to transplant, so besides rosemary and thyme and basil, the kinds of things we had at home in our spice cabinets, there were weird plants like wolfsbane, bloodwort, and nightshade. I felt like an apprentice witch.

Grandma stood behind me leaning on her cane. "Over there, Rhys. No. No. Farther to your right. You missed that weed. It's little now, but it will grow. No. No! Not that! That's a baby bay leaf. And you're stepping on the mint."

She stopped talking to me and started talking to the plants, as if reminding them what they were supposed to do too. "Oh, you tiny little thing. You've had too much sun, haven't you? All pale and burnt. I'll just have Rhys move you over by the bloodwort. Would you like that?"

I always knew what was coming next.

"Rhys, would you get the trowel from the wood shed? The green-handled one. We have to move the wolfs-bane."

I stabbed at the earth.

"A little deeper. Cup your hand under their little roots. Don't stand on the stem. They bleed too, you know. And you, thyme. You haven't grown a bit. Why go on living if you've stopped growing? Pull it, Rhys."

By the time I finished in the herb garden, the afternoon

paper had come. Unfortunately, Grandma's crossword puzzle was on the sports page.

Before I ever got to see the paper, dinner came and the dishes. I was the automatic dishwasher.

"Don't bother to dry them, Rhys. Scald them and leave them in the sink."

"But I don't like to see them piled in the drainer."

"It's more sanitary to scald them and let them dry."

It was the same every evening. Grandma didn't give in and neither did I. As soon as she left the kitchen, I dried the dishes and put them in the cupboard.

But the thing I hated worst were the sun porch windows. Twice a week I washed and polished them, inside and out, while Grandma pointed out the streaks—not all the porch windows, just the ones toward the lake.

"I never cared much about housekeeping, but my windows to the lake are always clean. A made-up bed is a silly luxury. Clear vision is a necessity."

After a week of Preston and Grandma, I was ready to go home.

"You're not having much fun, are you?" Mom stood in my bedroom doorway toweling her hair dry.

I was sitting up in bed reading the sports section and listening to records. Grandma was sleeping somewhere downstairs.

"Not exactly," I yawned. "But neither are you."

"No, I'm not. Sometimes I'd like to run away. Doesn't that sound awful?"

"No, it doesn't sound awful. Why don't we?"

"Why don't we what?" Mom's voice was muffled behind the towel.

"Run! We haven't done that together since we got here."

Mom pulled the towel down slowly so just her eyes were showing. "Oh, Rhys. What a wonderful idea. What would I do without you?"

"Get fat and lazy."

She threw the towel at me.

"Okay, kid. You've got a deal. Friday afternoon. Before dinner. I'll have the chapter finished. Think you can make it around the lake? It's eight miles."

"Think you can make it at Grandma's for the rest of the time? It's three weeks." I threw the towel back at her and flipped off the light. "If you can, I can."

"Rhys?" she called back.

"What, Mom?"

"Sleep well, honey."

Mom was neither fat nor lazy. I was reminded of that after we had jogged the first mile.

"Rhys and I thought we'd go for a run. Around the lake. Do you mind, Mother?" Mom had asked before we left.

Grandma peered at me over her reading glasses, her black eyes magnified. "Of course not. I don't suppose it ever occurred to you that I find my own company quite delightful. Off with you."

The afternoon was cool. Morning rain had left puddles on the blacktop. We ran through them, spraying each other with water. The road was flat and followed the shore past summer cabins, marinas, picnic grounds, and camp sites. A few weekend campers were beginning to arrive, but the only real sound was the rhythmic slap of our Adidas shoes against the blacktop.

At the beginning of what must have been the third mile, Mom slowed the pace. I was glad.

"I wouldn't mind stopping for a rest," Mom puffed. "Would you?"

"I sure wouldn't."

"Your grandmother's park is just ahead. About a quarter of a mile. Can you make it?"

"Can you?" I teased, picking up the pace.

It was my grandmother's park. At least there was a large sign with her name carved into the wood: Wyn Rhys State Park.

"How come it's named after her?"

Mom leaned back against a tree. "She gave the land to the state. It was hers from her father—a swamp, really, until they dredged it. She was on the governor's conservation board."

"I didn't know that. You never told me."

"I guess I never thought of it."

"What else have you forgotten?"

"A lot of things, I suppose. Things I forget to remember . . . until I come back home."

"Did you ever do stuff with her like we do? Not running . . . just being together and doing things?"

"Not really," Mom said, wiping the sweat from her forehead with the tail of her t-shirt. "It's hard to explain. She was a good mother. I was happy enough. But no. We didn't do many things like this."

"How come?"

"Because when we did, I didn't know what she wanted from me."

"Why didn't you ask her?"

"I don't know. Maybe I was afraid I couldn't do what she expected. You see, I thought she was perfect. I couldn't imagine her making a mistake. I used to envy Virene's children. Everyone in town thought Virene could never do anything right. A mother's one thing that you're stuck with. That holds true for you too, Rhys. I'm it. You can't trade me in on a better model."

"It goes both ways," I said, rubbing a cramp in my leg. "You're stuck with me for a daughter, you know."

"*Stuck* is the word, isn't it? Look at the two of us. Sitting in your grandmother's . . . my mother's park. I remember the day she gave it to the state, a hot July day. I was about a year younger than you are now and Father had died the winter before. Dave and I had to sit up on the platform right over there under that tree. I didn't want to, but Mother insisted. And she gave a speech. She had on this blue chiffon dress that I thought was the ugliest thing I had ever seen. I was embarrassed; I couldn't bear to look at her; I hated her that day. More to the point, I hated myself, I hated Dave, but I hated her most of all. I didn't know why, guess I still don't, except it was like being pulled two ways at once. Part of me wanted to get away from her and the other part wanted to run to her. I don't suppose I've been out to this park more than three or four times since that day."

"You make her sound so different. Not like now. Did she change?"

"No." Mom stood up and stretched. "I changed. Your grandmother is a private person. She's always lived in two worlds: her own, that no one ever shared, I think—and the world that included Dave and me. Some moments I almost broke through—when we almost touched, but I never knew what to say or do and the moment always passed. Now, when I almost understand, I can't do it."

"Do you need to?"

"Yes. To explain some things . . . to make her see me. But come on. We still have four miles to run."

We left the park, crossed the inlet bridge, fended off a yapping dog, and slowed down to a pace not much above a fast walk as the road curved around into a series of hills and ravines.

Mom moved ahead to set the pace, and I padded along three or four steps behind. I wondered, as I watched Mom, if she knew how much she was like Grandma. Everything she had said back at the park could have been said about her.

I remembered when she had to come over to our school to present some award at an assembly. I was so embarrassed. I couldn't even look at her. And talk about Grandma being private. No one could be as private as Mom.

"Here comes a car. Better get off on the shoulder," Mom called back.

"Probably heading out for Lover's Lane," I suggested.

"How do you know about Lover's Lane?"

"Every town has one, doesn't it?"

The car slowed and as it passed, the driver honked. I glanced over.

Sitting on the passenger side and waving a gloved hand was my grandmother. And beside her, driving . . . a man.

The car eased on down the road.

"Mom! Did you see! That was Grandma!"

Mom stopped and turned to look back. "Are you sure?"

"I'm sure. With some man."

Mom squinted back up the road.

"Who do you suppose she's with?" I asked.

35

"If it was a man, it was probably Reverend Baddeley."

"Who's he?"

"Her minister. They've known each other forever. Funny, though. She didn't say anything to me about his coming over. Or that she might enjoy a ride around the lake. I could have taken her."

I couldn't resist. I let out a whistle that sliced through the stillness of the tree-lined road. Mom turned and walked on down the road.

"I sure called that one wrong, didn't I?" I said slipping up beside her.

"What do you mean?"

"I said they were probably heading for Lover's Lane. I take it back. They're probably going out to Grandma's park to watch the grass grow."

"Rhys Ann." Mom clenched her teeth. "Sometimes you are exceedingly unfunny and extremely unoriginal."

We stopped to rest at the swimming beach before attempting the last half mile around the bay to Grandma's house. It was getting late: the water was empty except for a couple of kids out on the far diving tower.

"I sort of miss Kim," I said, watching the boy and girl race for the raft.

"My fault." Mom sighed. "You should have had a brother."

"Kim's better than a brother. He isn't around all the time. And he doesn't cost us anything."

"Except when he's around for breakfast, And lunch. And dinner."

"Did you like having a brother?"

"Dave was so much older. Eleven years. He was grown and gone before we became close."

"In a way, Mom, we're both only children."

"You did say *only*, didn't you?"

"Yes."

"I thought you might have said *lonely*."

When we got home, Grandma was on the porch . . . alone.

"Did you have a good time on your run?" she asked. She looked relaxed. Maybe it had been as good for her to get out of the house as it had been for Mom and me.

Mom sat on the footstool, and I stretched out on the couch.

"We had fun. We stopped at your park, just before we met you."

"Yes. We stopped there too. It was lovely. And so thoughtful of Wid to drop in and take me for a ride."

"Wid?" I asked.

"Reverend Baddeley," Mom explained. "How is he, Mother? I haven't seen him for years."

"He never changes. Even with all those honors and books and high offices. Strange, isn't it, that he decided to come back to Preston and our church."

"Nice for you. Does he have a family?" Mom asked.

"His wife is dead. His children grown and gone."

"It's funny," Mom said, "the bits and pieces you remember from childhood. Reverend Baddeley. A deep, rumbling voice. And he smelled like tobacco and shaving lotion."

"I'm surprised you recall that much. You were only four when he left. Can you remember the time you and I went out tricks-and-treating? You were a ghost and I was a witch, and we went up to the parsonage door and Wid had no idea who we were.

"I don't remember that. It must have been you and Dave."

"When Dave was little I couldn't get him out of the house on Halloween. He was scared of the dark."

"I was afraid of the dark too."

"Oh, Eve. You couldn't have been. You were always the strong one. But Dave . . ." Her voice trailed off.

"What about Uncle Dave?" I asked.

"Well, he wasn't weak. But he needed so much reassurance." She turned to Mom. "But you. I could always count on you, Eve."

"For what?"

"For understanding. For understanding how important you were."

Mom's head moved as if in slow motion and she looked at Grandma. "I didn't know you thought I was important. You never told me that."

"I don't suppose I ever did. But certainly you knew. Not everything has to be put into words."

"Words might have changed things, Mother. I might have understood what you wanted me to be."

"Be! I wanted you to be yourself. I didn't want to smother you. Most of all I didn't want a clone of me. A child needs room to grow."

"Maybe I had too much room." Mom reached down, untied her shoelaces, and kicked off her sneakers." "But that's all past. Besides, I need a shower."

Grandma turned to me, her face flushed. "Your mother, Rhys, is a good runner."

"Well," Mom said, standing up. "Good runners take showers and Rhys had better too if she expects to eat with us. What shall we have for dinner?"

"Leftovers," Grandma said, staring out across the lake.

5

Three Generations

We had become a tense household, Grandma, Mom and I—a pyramid of age locked into one house.

One night I looked out my sleeping porch window. Mom was in her swimsuit, sitting at the end of the dock. All I could see was her silhouette against the darkening water, and there was a slump to her usually straight shoulders. I figured I was part of it. Since coming to Grandma's, I had gotten in the habit of jumping on things Mom said and either arguing the point or offering a likely substitute. Even though I promised myself I wouldn't do it again, I always did.

I wondered if Mom wanted to be alone or if she were lonely.

"Your mother is a private person, Rhys," Grandma had told me once down by the herb garden. I was weeding and she was lying back in the chaise longue.

"I remember one Christmas. The house was full of

people. Relatives, friends and all their children. And it was noisy and crowded. It was time for Eve to go to bed, and I couldn't find her. I suppose she was around three. I found her hiding under the piano, with her toys around her. 'What are you doing there?' I asked. 'Wouldn't you like some cake and milk before you go to bed?' And that little smidgin of a girl looked up at me and said, *'Don't boffer me!'* And I didn't. She still gets that 'don't-boffer-me' look about her."

I knew Mom's look too, but that night I pulled on my swimsuit and tiptoed downstairs anyway. Grandma was asleep in her chair on the porch. Had she heard me, she'd have called out her usual question that sounded more like a reprimand: "You leaving?"

Mom heard me as I stepped on the dock. "Is anything wrong?"

"No. That's what I was going to ask you." I tried not to sound tired of hearing that question which had become her only greeting.

She shifted and made room for me. "No. Nothing's wrong, I guess."

I dangled my feet in the water. The lake was still, the sky black behind a sprinkling of stars, the air silky.

"What are you doing down here all by yourself?"

"Just remembering. You know the Welsh believed that water bewitches people, and if the wind throws spray on you, you could be sucked into the depths. Dave and I were the best swimmers in Preston. Your grandmother scared us into swimming."

"She didn't really believe that, did she?"

"Half-believed, maybe. The lake is alive to her. I'd come down for breakfast and she'd say, 'look how beautiful Lady Lake is this morning.' Nature is special to her.

40

In the spring we'd always have to go wren hunting.
There was a song she sang:

> The wrens are scarce
> They've flown away
> But they'll come back
> When fair folk play.

"And you found wrens?"

"Always. She cried when they chopped down our
birch tree in front to widen the street. She called birches
trees of love." Mom slipped into the water. "Come on
in. It's lovely."

It was and we were not pulled into the depths. We
floated on our backs, bewitched by the night sky.

"It's not like home, is it?" I said, diving down and
surfacing beside her.

"Not for you. It is for me. Only it's sad, now."

"You can't go home again. We read a book about that
last year in school," I said and hoisted myself up on the
dock.

Mom swam out a few yards, did a submerged racing
turn and came back, her movement hardly rippling the
surface. Mom had a beautiful crawl that I could never
quite match.

"Grandma taught you to swim?"

Mom clung to the pier post with one hand and floated
beside the dock. "Yes. She taught Dave and me, right off
this pier. Everything she did came so naturally. I don't
think she ever had to work to learn anything. Not that I
was in competition. . . ."

She dog-paddled around to the other side of the dock.

"On the other hand, maybe all daughters are in competition with their mothers. And a daughter is never free until . . ."

"Until?" I repeated.

She planted her palms on the dock and with one twist was sitting beside me. "Until they're orphaned. Or grown up enough to realize there was no contest after all."

"Personally, I don't think I ever want to be a mother," I said, churning the water into waves with my feet. "I don't want to be somebody's caretaker all my life."

"You aren't the first sixteen-year old who's said that, and you probably won't be the last."

She shook her head, sprinkling me with lake water.

"To tell you the truth, I was sitting out here wondering when it gets to be *my* turn. Here I am. Forty-two years old. I've spent all my life being a daughter and half my life being a mother. When do I get to be *me*?"

I didn't have an answer.

"I'm afraid if we stay here with your grandmother much longer we'll devour each other."

"Oh, Mom!" and I meant it to sound just the way it came out. "It can't be that bad."

"It's how I feel." She stretched out flat on her back, resting her head on her hands, and stared into the sky. "Maybe a mother loves from instinct, and a daughter loves from duty. Or, what if it's not love at all? Just habit."

Water lapped softly against the pier.

I turned and looked down into my mother's face. She might have been no older than I. Her eyes were closed, and her hair curled in damp wisps across her forehead.

"Do me a favor, Mom. Be any age you want, but not forty-two. It's too depressing."

Mom usually laughed at my attempts to be clever. This time she didn't.

"I *am* forty-two. And I'm not talking about us. I'm talking about your grandmother and me."

There was something wrong with Mom's logic.

"Don't you love Grandma?"

Mom didn't answer right away.

"I might love her more easily if she weren't my mother."

She sat up, her shoulder brushing mine.

"But I'd love you either way, mother or not." I said.

She picked up her towel and we started for the house.

"Rhys, I'm not sure everything I said was true. I might have exaggerated. Coming back here to Mother's has made me feel like a child again. All the old questions, the old doubts, the old expectations. Oh, Rhys. You understand what I mean. I don't have to spell it out to you." She hugged me.

She was wrong, of course.

We walked back to the house together.

Grandma was standing in the porch window waiting for us.

"Wouldn't some *Pice Ar y Maen* taste good? With milk?" her eyes brightened.

"What's that?" I asked.

"Welsh cakes. You remember, Eve?"

Grandma already had the mixing bowl out on the counter.

"Come, sit down."

We sat while Grandma measured, poured, sifted, sampled, greased, and floured.

"Never could have done this in that nursing home."

She stood at the stove and we watched as she ladled batter into skillet. "They program you. Television time. Bath time. Meal time. Craft time. Rest time. Sing time. Visit time." She turned the cake to brown on the other side. "Then they put you to bed like children and pill you to sleep. I get my best ideas at night. I love the night. Such a shame to sleep it away. Worst of all," Grandma scooped the cake from pan to plate, wiped her hands on a towel, and sat down with us. "There's so little left in a place like that for laughter. The only things you can laugh about are so sad there's no room for tears."

"What do you mean, Mother?" Mom asked quietly.

"Well. Hattie Daniels. She slept a lot. All the time, in fact. In front of the TV, during visiting hours and sometimes she'd even drift off over her plate at dinner. Poor soul. She was so bored. One Sunday afternoon they wheeled me out to the reception room and parked me beside Hattie. Her son and daughter-in-law were visiting, and they kept making conversation and she kept dropping off. Finally the daughter-in-law reached over and shook Hattie's shoulder. 'Hattie, dear, wake up. Aren't you glad to see us?' Hattie opened her eyes, looked straight at the two of them and said, 'Like hell I am!' and promptly went back to sleep."

Mom and I both laughed. Grandma did too, but there were tears behind our laughter.

6

Thinning Out

The Virene-less week turned into two. Grandma got a postcard with a picture of a huge, technicolor fish jumping from the water. All it said was, "Buell and I had no luck here. We'll try farther north." Life smoothed out, and after the Welsh Cakes, the tension eased. Mom was making progress on her dissertation, Grandma was having less trouble walking, and I played golf every day. Of course I was playing by myself, but I didn't mind.

Golf is like anything you really care about: reading, painting, writing. It's nice if you can share, but if you can't, the thing itself is important enough.

At home I played on an eighteen-hole course. Preston's was only nine-hole, so I had to play around twice. Some mornings I played the inside first and the outside five last. Then the next day, I'd play the outside five and end with the inside four.

One hot morning, I finished off my eighteen holes with

a fairly decent score and decided to get a Coke before starting the bike ride home. The pro shop wasn't really a pro shop. They had balls and clubs and stuff for sale, but mostly it was a bar and lunch counter, all run by one person.

This one person unfolded his long legs from the bar stool, put down a book he was reading, and went behind the counter. I was his only customer.

"Help you?" he asked, half-bored, as if I'd interrupted his reading.

"A Coke."

He was tall, but not too tall, muscular, but not like a weight lifter, tanned, his hair sun-bleached. As a matter of fact, he was gorgeous.

"Hot out there?" he reached under the counter, snapped off the cap and set a Coke bottle before me.

"Hot!" I answered, wishing I could think of something clever to say.

I tipped up the Coke and glanced at his book.

"Poetry? Yeats?"

He planted his hands on the counter in front of me and looked at me for the first time. "Only on Wednesdays."

"Only on Wednesdays?" I repeated. I didn't usually have trouble talking with people, but now when I wanted to sound intelligent, my words came out like a five-year-old's.

"Sure. I read Westerns on Thursdays." He was perfectly serious.

"I suppose you read comic books on Fridays?" It wasn't too sharp but at least it was a complete sentence.

"Wrong!" he said with a swipe of his bar rag. "I don't read on Fridays."

46

"What do you do on Fridays?" I tried to say it casually as if I didn't really care.

"Friday's my day off. I fish."

"Really? I didn't know the lake was good for fishing."

"Who knows? I don't use a hook." He leaned against the counter on one elbow. I hurriedly took several swallows of my Coke.

"I refuse to ask why you go fishing without a hook." He was obviously much older than I, probably in college.

"I wouldn't ask either." He grinned. "But I'll tell you anyway. I like to get in a boat, row out around the Point and just sit and drift. Without a fishing pole, people'd think I was crazy."

It made some kind of sense. I could feel him looking at me. I hope he liked what he saw.

"You play a lot of golf, don't you? I've seen you out here before."

"Not much else to do in Preston."

"I don't suppose."

A golf cart purred to a stop just outside the door, and a woman about my mother's age came into the shop. "Have you any golf balls guaranteed to go one hundred yards on every drive?"

My newly-discovered gorgeous man motioned to the back display case. "No guarantee on distance, but I guarantee they're all round."

"Maybe that's my trouble," the woman said, curling her legs around the bar stool and resting her elbows on the counter. "I bet I've been using a square ball."

"Now, Midge. You know what I keep telling you. You've got to keep your eye on the ball."

"I know. I know. That's the painful part. Watching

where it goes—in the water, in the rough, in the sand trap."

I sipped slowly, trying to make my drink last until the woman left.

"Let me finish up in here, and I'll meet you out on the first tee and help you."

I figured I was part of his "finish-up-in-here" chore, so I drained the last swallow and set the bottle down on the counter.

"You live here in town?" he asked me, as the woman left.

"Just visiting."

"Stop in some morning. I usually get out here early. I'll play a round or two with you."

"But not on Friday?"

He laughed. "You're right. Not on Friday. I putt my best on Tuesdays. Try Tuesday."

"Try Tuesday! Try Tuesday!" I repeated as I biked home. I would definitely try Tuesday. I had never realized what a lovely day Tuesday could be. I didn't even know his name. It didn't matter. He was handsome. He was intelligent. He was funny. He was older! I wouldn't say anything to Mom. I'd write to Kim. He'd understand.

In the last year, Kim and I had spent a lot of time talking about what it felt like to be growing up and specifically about dating and sex. There wasn't much we didn't know about each other's fantasies. Maybe that was why our talking was never embarrassing. Of course, sex wasn't the only thing we talked about, but as Kim said, "It is important. It is a part of life."

We both wondered how and when we'd know it was

the right person and the right time. We were sure that, because it was important, it should be special.

We decided the ultimate test would be if we could use that person's toothbrush. Then the relationship would be special.

The man in the pro shop had perfectly beautiful teeth.

The house was quiet when I got back, except for the muted clicking of Mom's typewriter from her upstairs study. I wandered through the kitchen and out to the sun porch, tucking the pro shop man firmly in the back of my mind. I still wasn't quite sure that Grandma's eyes couldn't see right through me.

The couch was covered with garment boxes and tissue paper, and Grandma was holding a flowered blouse at arm's length, studying it carefully.

"Packing or unpacking?" I asked.

"I'm shopping. I had Taylor's send out some things on approval. I'm beginning to feel dowdy. My old clothes hang like sacks. Do you like this?"

"It's nice. What else did you get?"

"I haven't decided yet. I could get by with just one outfit, but you know what, Rhys? I have a feeling I'm going to keep them all. Nothing like a new outfit to make you feel human. Makes you know you've got a body that's alive." I knew exactly what she meant, but for me it didn't have anything to do with clothes. I did wonder why Grandma thought she needed new things. She'd only been out of the house once since we came.

"What about this one? I like it, but not for me. It's more like something you'd wear. Try it on."

She held up a sporty blue blazer. I looked at the label. "I couldn't get into that. It's only a size eight."

"It is, isn't it? Used to wear size twelve," and she looked at me as if she were going to say something more and then changed her mind, and added, turning away, "That's the way it goes. Spend half a lifetime growing and half a lifetime shrinking."

She took the blazer from me, folded it and placed it back into its box, the tissue paper rustling under her hands.

"You know," she said, patting the box shut. "I believe I'm going to ask your mother to sort through my old clothes and take them down to Good Will. I've stuff up there I'll never wear again. A person's got to do the same things with life as with carrots—thin it out eventually. I'm reaching the thinning stage. I might decide to have an auction after all."

"You'd better break it to Mom gently, Grandma. She'll flip out if she has to call that auctioneer again."

"Don't underestimate your mother, Rhys. Daughters sometimes do."

The next afternoon I was home with Grandma while Mom did grocery shopping, returned the blue blazer, and stopped in the library to pick up the latest best seller for Grandma.

I didn't hear the doorbell ring, but I did hear footsteps in the hall.

"Wyn!" a voice called. "Where are you?"

"Where would I be?" Grandma answered. "On my porch, of course."

I turned to see a big man, broad-shouldered, a shock of iron gray hair falling across his forehead.

"You must be Rhys. You look exactly like your grandmother. But I'm sure you know that. I'm Wid Baddeley."

"He's also a minister." Grandma sighed, moving toward her favorite chair. "But it's too late for him to remedy that now."

Grandma was wearing the new flowered blouse from Taylor's.

He sat down beside her without invitation, leaned over, and kissed her cheek. "How's my Welsh witch today?"

"Eternal." A period punctuated the dip of her voice.

"Better than infernal." He leaned back and folded his arms. "What I need is some of your herb tea."

"What is medicine for the Welsh is poison for the English. Bring him some, Rhys."

He threw back his head and laughed. It was not a ministerial laugh. It was not a polite laugh. It was a raucous laugh.

"Can I look forward to seeing you and Virene in church next Sunday? It's conference Sunday."

I brought a pitcher of Grandma's herb tea.

"You know," he said turning to me, "they attend my church only on the dullest Sundays of the year. On purpose, I'm sure. Just to see me at my worst."

Grandma laughed in delight. "We go when we know he's going to have an empty house. Conference Sundays when he tells me how he's wasting my pew rent. Fourth of July if it falls on Sunday and always the Sunday after Easter."

"It's better than not having you there at all." The laughter left his voice.

"Come sit down and join us, Rhys," Grandma suggested. "After all, Preston isn't overrun with ministers. Only two: Reverend Wright. He's Congregational. And Reverend Baddeley here. And you can depend on one

51

thing. Wright does Baddeley, and Baddeley does Wright. Every chance they get."

I made a face.

Reverend Baddeley smiled at me. "Your grandmother has an evil sense of humor. She's a reprobate, you know. I never could convert her."

"I think, Rhys, he uses 'reprobate' to mean 'abandoned!'" Grandma smiled sweetly at him. "So if I'm abandoned, why don't you leave me, Wid?"

He took a long swallow of the tea and raised his glass to her. "Oh Wyn. Who else ever lifted my spirits the way you do?" He looked at me. "Your grandmother and I have known each other for years. We have totally different ideas on life—as well as what happens afterwards. We've a running bet as to who is right."

"Our only problem is," Grandma chuckled, "how does either one of us collect the bet? I'm ten years older, so it concerns me more. But I told him, Rhys, if, after I'm dead, he should find a three-dollar bill in his collection plate some Sunday morning, he'd know who won."

"I'd rather go first and let you win." He seemed to have forgotten I was in the room.

"Don't pay any attention to us, Rhys," Grandma said. "We don't mean half what we say."

"Or say half what we mean," Reverend Baddeley added quietly, and Grandma turned and gazed out the window and did not challenge his words.

Their gentle battle continued as long as the pitcher of tea lasted.

The minister finally stood up, swished the remaining tea around in the bottom of his glass, looked down at my grandmother and said, "You know, Wyn, the last sip is the sweetest," and he tipped up his glass.

Grandma turned away. "I hope so," she murmured.

Reverend Baddeley left without saying good-bye.

When he was gone, Grandma asked me to carry a lawn chair down by her herb garden. "I need some space," she explained, and she sat in the shade the rest of the afternoon studying the lake and talking to her plants, the Welsh mixed in with the English: "*Gwallt y Forwyn, bach.* So sturdy. Remember how pale you were when I found you? *Ymenyn Tylwyth Teg.* That's what does it, *Tylwyth Teg.* Fairy butter. Growing is painful. Wilting is much easier."

Then there were times when I thought she was talking to herself rather than the plants.

"*Amser i blannu, ac amser i dynnu y peth a blannwyd.*"

"What does that mean?"

She had not noticed me standing beside her.

"It means a time to plant and a time to pluck out the things which were planted."

7

Fairy Butter

"Wynnie!" Virene exploded through the front door. "I've got a whole mess of walleyes out in the camper. Dropped Buell off at the truck stop and came right over. You know what I'm going to do? I'm going to fry up a mess of these fish and we're going to have a picnic tonight, in your backyard."

If it were the mystical power of Grandma's "fairy butter" that made her herbs flourish (she never did tell me exactly what fairy butter was, but I think it was some kind of moss) Virene provided the "fairy butter" for Grandma.

"Now, Wynnie, get yourself fixed up. I'll make an appointment with Marg for you to have your hair done. Eve can take you."

When Vi was around, Grandma sat up straighter, her color was better, she laughed more, and she talked: a flood of words and broken sentences punctuated with chuckles. I almost expected the old Twtti Wyn Hec to appear again and dance around the kitchen with a broom.

"And say, Wyn. Mind if I bring my youngest grand-son along?"

"Lew? Bring him along by all means. And, Eve, run down to the store and buy some white wine. Buy three bottles while you're at it. We're going to have a celebration. Rhys, pick some flowers after you move the picnic table up into the shade. I've just the thing to wear, Vi. I've been shopping."

"Good, Wynnie. I'll throw together a salad."

Grandma stood up, her cane forgotten. "And I'll make my fish sauce, Vi. You know that special one you like so well."

While Mom drove to the store, I went down to the picnic table. Vi and Grandma were still planning the picnic as if they were catering a banquet.

"Rhys!" Grandma called from the back door. "Don't forget those flowers when you move the picnic table. Get the red peonies over there by the border of the house—and some honeysuckle."

Mom came back with the wine—all three bottles.

"Put them in the refrigerator, Rhys," Mom said. "I imagine your grandmother likes it very cold. If you'll see that everything is set up outside, I'll help in here. And, dear, I hope you don't mind keeping your eye on Vi's grandson. We don't want to tire your grandmother. I hate to make you babysit, but maybe you could take him for a walk along the lake, after we eat. I think there's still a bunch of poles in the basement. Maybe you could take him fishing."

"Sure," I agreed reluctantly.

Everything was ready long in advance of the picnic hour, so I curled up with a book in one of the lawn chairs.

The backyard did look festive. Grandma had had Mom get out all the lawn furniture from the basement. Of course it all had to be hosed down and wiped off and arranged just so.

I heard the back door slam, and I looked up to see my grandmother walking down the steps. I gasped, not because she was without her cane. I gasped at *her*. She was beautiful in a cardinal red pantsuit and white blouse. Her hair, a spun halo of white, framed dancing black eyes—Grandma seldom wore her glasses.

I heard Vi's Lincoln Continental grind to a stop in the drive. As I squinted into the sun, intensified now by the reflection from the old white house, in a weird flash it was as if I were seeing my grandmother the way she must have looked as a young girl, coming down the same steps.

"They're here," Mom called from the kitchen. "Rhys, would you get the mosquito repellent? We may need it."

I unwrapped myself from the lawn chair and tossed down my book. Grandma looked up as I walked past. "Every picnic has to have a go-fer, and I guess you're our go-fer."

"I know." I smiled back, still with the eerie feeling I was seeing someone other than my grandma.

"You've got the young legs. Someday you can order others around."

"If I live long enough," I said.

Grandma snorted.

I came out of the house just as Virene rounded the corner. "We're here!" she shouted and motioned to someone behind her. "Set that down, Lew. There at the end of the table."

She gave Grandma a quick hug. "This is my grandson, Lew. You remember Wyn, and that's Eve, and there's a Rhys around here some place."

I stopped halfway through the door.

It was the person from the pro shop, the reader of Yeats on Wednesday.

"Rhys! You look different without a golf club." His eyes were teasing. "I've never known a Rhys before."

"Neither have I," I answered, feeling three pairs of older eyes lift at once and zero in on me.

"What's up with you two?" Virene asked. "Do you know each other?"

"Sure." Lew answered for me. "We've got a date for a round of golf tomorrow morning, haven't we?" He came over and took the can of repellent.

"You didn't tell me, Rhys," exclaimed my mother. I glanced past her to my grandmother.

"Tell you, Eve!" Grandma sputtered. "Since when have daughters told their mothers everything?"

"That fish ought to go in the oven, Lew." Vi shifted the conversation.

"Here, I'll show you," Mom offered. "Should I open the wine, Mother?"

"That would be nice."

I escaped the detailed explanation about meeting Lew and my golf date.

He picked up the pan of fish and followed Mom into the house.

"I can fix some cheese and crackers," I offered, a bit too eagerly.

Grandma raised her eyebrows. "I think wine will be enough," she said, patting the chair beside her, and I sat like an obedient dog. "My, Virene, he's turned into a handsome young man. It's been years since I've seen him."

"He's going to be a doctor. Imagine me having a doctor in the family. I never made it through high school and Corine, his mother, didn't do any better."

"Hope they teach him something besides pill-pushing," Grandma added. "You didn't tell me he was coming to visit you."

"I wasn't sure when he was coming. I told him last winter he could have the job. You see, Rhys, I own the concession stand. One of my nephews filled in for him until he got here. Lew's a good boy. I have a whole pack of grandkids, but I must admit, he's my favorite."

"How old is he?" I asked, trying to be nonchalant.

"Twenty-six. Too old for you, Rhys. Too young for your mother. Just the right age for Wyn and me." Vi guffawed, and Grandma giggled.

Just as I was thinking it was taking Mom an awfully long time in the kitchen, they came out, Lew balancing a tray of wine and glasses, and Mom carrying a plate of . . . cheese and crackers! Maybe it was the shadows, but in her t-shirt and shorts, Mom didn't look too old for Lew. And Lew didn't look too young for Mom!

We sat in a circle, and Lew poured the wine.

"A toast. To grandmothers, mothers and granddaughters." He raised his glass.

"And grandsons," Grandma added.

"To all of us, then," he agreed, and we sipped our wine.

"When do you finish your course work, Lew?" Mom began.

"In the fall," he replied turning toward her. "You'll have your doctorate long before I'm a doctor. It's partly

Wyn's fault, you know. When I was a kid she got me interested in that herb garden of hers." He swung around. "Remember, Wyn?"

Grandma sat up straighter in her chair. "Of course, I remember. I had you over here mowing my lawn, and you clipped off all my rosemary."

"Yes. And you grabbed me by the collar, sat me down, and taught me the name of every plant. I can still say the names: *Gwallt y Forwyn, Helyg Mair, Cennin Pedr.*"

"You got the Welsh right, but your accent is wretched," Grandma teased.

"You've got to admit, Wyn, it's not bad for an Irish-Italian. And that," Lew said, turning toward his grandmother, "is your fault."

"Now look here. You can't blame me for my parents, boy."

I must have looked bewildered because Virene leaned toward me. "See, Rhys, Momma was Irish, her name was Irene. And Poppa was Italian, and his name was Vincent. Put them together and you get Virene. And that's just what happened."

At least Virene was including me in the conversation.

"You sit over there, Rhys, with Virene." Mom pointed to the opposite side of the picnic table as she slipped in beside Lew. Grandma sat on the other side of Lew.

I felt as if someone had taken my playground swing away from me and I wanted to shout, "He's mine! I saw him first!" I *had* found him first out at the golf course. Wasn't I going to play a round of golf with him? Didn't they know he was interested in me? He'd asked *me.* What right did Mom have to take over? And Grandma was no better, sitting close to him and dropping her hand casually on his arm to gain his attention.

"You say"—Mom held the salad bowl as Lew forked out lettuce for her and then for himself—"that you have only your lab work to finish in microbiology and then . . ."

I felt an ugly enmity toward both the older women sitting across from me. "Did Midge finally find a ball that would stay on the fairway?" I broke in.

Mom looked at me as if she'd forgotten I was there.

"After about ten tries and as many whiffs." Lew passed the salad bowl on to Grandma. "Salad, Wyn?"

"Oh, yes, thank you. Rhys, you interrupted your mother. What were you saying, Eve?"

Vi shoved a bowl of Grandma's tartar sauce under my nose. "Try some of this on your fish, Rhys."

I ate my fish, covered with Grandma's sauce, in silence.

"Well, I was saying," Mom went on with a significant emphasis on the "was," "that if you have that much done this summer, Lew, you should be looking around for an internship before long."

"Never thought my herb garden would produce a doctor." Grandma interrupted, but Mom didn't seem to notice.

"Try some more fish, Rhys." Vi passed the platter.

"Fish always reminds me," Grandma said, "of a story my father used to tell . . ."

"Oh, Mother," Mom sighed. "Not that one."

Grandma ignored her. "An old Welsh woman was gathering shells down by the ocean. Her wedding ring slipped off and a big wave washed it out to sea. She searched and searched and searched. She finally gave up and went home, fearing to tell her husband. You can imagine how she felt. Well . . ." Grandma paused dramatically, "the next day a fisherman came around selling

60

fresh herring, and she bought one. When she cleaned the fish, what do you think she found inside?"

"The ring?" Lew asked as if prompted.

"No!" Grandma beamed. "The guts!"

"Oh, Mother." Mom coughed a short laugh.

Virene laughed so hard the picnic table bounced. Lew laughed the loudest.

I swallowed a mouthful of fish wishing it had been salad.

"Rhys, why don't you go up and get the dessert?" Mom didn't bother to look at me. What I heard was, "You are still a child."

Grandma looked up from her plate. "Go-fer," she whispered and winked.

During dessert, Lew talked about golf, Mom talked about her research, Virene talked about her fishing trip and Grandma talked about her herbs.

I didn't talk.

Virene cleared the table, and I offered to help, but Grandma said, "Rhys has done her share. Why don't you take Lew down and show him how nice my new herb plantings are doing? The ones you set out for me."

I could have hugged her.

"Perhaps Lew would be more interested in that special that's on TV," Mom suggested. "Didn't you mention something, Lew?"

"It really doesn't matter. A walk might feel good."

He didn't invite Mother to come along.

I could have hugged *him*.

Not talking, we walked down across the lawn, past Grandmother's herb garden, to the path that wound around the lake shore. Our silence wasn't uneasy, and that was strange, at least for me. Mom and Kim had always been the only two people with whom I felt comfortable being quiet.

Lew smelled good. I don't mean he was wearing cologne or anything, but I could smell him the way you can smell cotton candy at a carnival—kind of sweet and exciting. Or maybe it was that I wanted to soak him up, so I imagined more than was real.

We stopped at the playground. There weren't any kids around.

"Let's try the merry-go-round."

I swallowed twice. I sat on the edge, clutching the iron rail. How could I tell him that going in circles made me sick to my stomach—instantly. He gave a push and jumped on beside me.

"I hope you don't mind going slow. Merry-go-rounds make me sick."

"Me too," I agreed, dragging my feet to slow us even more. "And so does fish. I think it's the bones."

"I know. For me it's the skin lurking there under the breading—black and silver and slimy—even if I can't see it."

"Gross!" I said.

"There should be a special kind of fish. Somebody should grow some without bones or skin."

"Grow some? Gruesome. What could we name the fish?"

"A gross!" Lew dug his feet into the sand and the merry-go-round stopped. "Look. There's fish named groupers and birds named grouse. So why not a fish named gross?"

"Sort of like a net gross?"

"That's awful, Rhys."

"You know what a gross looks like? Like a fast-food hamburger—and it just floats along the top of the water . . ."

"Yeah," Lew added, "and sucks in lettuce, mustard and ketchup."

"And it lives in a sesame seed bun."

Lew pretended to choke and fell back on the platform. "Come on, you can do better than that. Listen. It's a fish native to this lake only, and immune to Buell's or Virene's lures."

"Oh," I said, thanking my junior high librarian. "You mean a fish gross in Preston like *A Tree Grows in Brooklyn?*"

We began laughing at each other and ourselves so hard that we couldn't stop. After a while my stomach *did* begin to hurt, and I guess Lew's did too. He reached around the rail and we hung onto each other until the last of the laughter left. We lay together, gasping, and looking into each other's eyes.

"Come on," Lew said slowly. "We're supposed to be taking a walk."

So we walked, and walked, and walked. Then we walked some more—down to the swimming beach, in front of the summer cabins, behind East End Restaurant, and out to the point.

We finally found a picnic table and sat down across from each other. "We don't have to go back right away, do we?" he asked. "We can stay and listen to the night."

It was the most poetic thing anyone had ever said to me. I wondered if he knew how old I was. Somehow, I didn't think it mattered.

"Funny, isn't it?" Lew began. "That we're both here

63

this summer with our grandmothers. Do you know what the chances are of something like that happening? Meeting each other, I mean."

I nodded, thoughts of Colorado melting from my mind. "Grandmothers are wonderful," I answered, not thinking of grandmothers at all, but watching his mouth.

"Rhys . . ." He stopped and brushed a leaf from the table. "Rhys, you're really something. Maybe it sounds phony, but, somehow, we fit—you and I."

I knew exactly what he meant. I'd known it from our first conversation in the pro shop. I also knew, or thought I knew, that things like this didn't happen very often.

I stretched my arm across the table, my hand palm up.

He curled his little finger around mine. "Make a wish," he said.

It was not hard to make a wish.

He released my hand. I think we both were a little embarrassed. I mean we didn't know each other very well and I'm sure that neither of us expected the closeness we were feeling. I know it sounds dramatic, but I was feeling something a lot like love.

A whirr of wings stirred the trees above us.

"Herons," Lew whispered, almost reverently. "They've come up from the reserve. Can you see them—up there in the top?"

"They're beautiful," I whispered back. And they were. Not like the awkward birds that stood around the shore, but like something out of Greek mythology, strong and graceful, as they soared into the branches.

"You are too, Rhys."

"Too what?" I jumped to the kind of kidding Kim and I did. I wished I hadn't.

"Beautiful," he repeated. "You are beautiful too."

I didn't know what to do with the words. They hung between us. For the first time I could remember, even with Kim or Mom or my father, I didn't have an answer.

Slowly, hand in hand, we walked back to Grandma's house. Virene had gone home. Grandma was in bed, and Mom was sitting out on the lawn. She had never paid much attention to what time I came in when Kim and I were together.

"I thought you were taking a walk. You've been gone long enough for a back-packing excursion."

"Mother!" I hated the way I sounded.

"It was my fault, Eve." Lew patted her shoulder. "We walked over to the point. A flock of blue herons were in the trees. I guess we lost track of time."

It was true. We'd watched until they flew back to the reserve, and then we sat on the bank as the sky darkened and we tried to identify the constellations.

I didn't see why I had to explain. After all, she was my mother and should have understood.

Lew was practicing on the putting green when I got to the club house the next morning. He didn't hear the crunch of my bike tires, so I stood and watched him. He *was* the handsomest man I'd ever met, but even better, I really liked him and he didn't seem to care about the gap in our ages or else he hadn't noticed.

I leaned my bicycle against the clubhouse as Lew rolled a perfect twenty-footer into the cup.

"Who couldn't putt better on Tuesday after an hour on the practice green?" I called. "That isn't fair."

"Who said I play fair?"

It didn't take long for me to see that Lew was also a gorgeous golfer. He showed me what was wrong with my short approaches. I wasn't lining up with my left foot. That's what's interesting about golf: you can't see your own weaknesses, but someone else can watch you and see them right away.

You have to concentrate to play a good game of golf, so neither of us talked much until we decided to rest before starting the long ninth hole: a 595-yarder, a dog leg with two creeks and a ring of sand traps around the green.

I was trying to think of something to say that would steer us to a personal level. I didn't have the chance.

"You have an interesting family, Rhys. Your grandmother's a fascinating woman."

I wasn't particularly interested in talking about Grandma, but I decided it didn't really matter because I just liked the sound of his voice: deep and soft like velvet.

"I hadn't seen her since I was twelve or so, but I never forgot her. When I was a kid, Virene sent me over every Saturday morning to see if there was anything Wyn needed. There always was. I never minded, though, because she'd talk to me as if I were an adult. I suppose it sounds silly, but I think I was half in love with her. She had a way of making me feel special."

"I don't really know her . . . very well. At least not since I've grown up. There's a lot about her I don't understand. Neither does Mom."

"I'd like to get to know your mother better, too. Too bad you're going to be here for such a short time."

I remembered what Mom had said about competition between mothers and daughters. I was beginning to believe her. She might have included grandmothers, too. The projected affair with Lew that I'd mentioned in the letter I'd written to Kim last night seemed less probable.

"What about granddaughters?"

"I'm not sure," Lew said, standing up and selecting a wood. "But I'm finding out." He walked over to the tee without looking back. His drive lit well beyond the 200-yard marker.

When we got back to the pro shop, a foursome was waiting to tee off. The women, all older than I, descended upon Lew like hungry ants at a picnic.

"Want to play again tomorrow?" he asked over his shoulder as he hurried into the shop.

I certainly did.

"We're going to start with the attic," Grandma announced that morning when I got back from the golf course. "Lew's promised to come over after work and carry the boxes down to the porch for me. There's a lot to go through."

I would see Lew again. The words repeated themselves over and over in my head like a song, "Lew-again, Lew-again."

"Are you sure you want to start? It's a big undertaking," Mom said, and I was sure I knew what she was thinking. We'd be going home in another week or so and Grandma would be going back to the nursing home. How could Uncle Dave possibly put the house on the market again if Grandma had her stuff scattered all over? I also knew what I was thinking—that I was in no hurry to leave Preston after all.

Before Mom and I knew it, we were trotting up and down stairs from the attic, carrying the "little stuff." Grandma did have the power to make people do things whether they were eager or not.

"What are we going to do?" Mom asked as we struggled, arms full, down the steep attic steps. "We have to leave for home soon, and I can't seem to make her understand."

"She's *your* mother," I shrugged. "I have one of my own to handle."

"If my hands weren't full, I'd paddle you." She laughed.

Grandma sat on the porch, directing the placement of the boxes.

"Oh, those are Christmas cards. Put them over by the door. I'll burn those. Now the box of photographs I want here on the table."

We carried for two hours, but when it came to Grandma's "sorting out" we didn't get past the box of photographs.

"Now, this was my father and mother, Evan and Caiwen Rhys. They met on the boat coming over from Wales. Couldn't speak a word of English. I didn't learn English until I started school."

I looked at the fresh young faces in the faded pictures. I knew a part of me was there somewhere, but I could not find it. It was hard to believe there was anyone before Grandma.

"You carry their name, Rhys."

She had used the right word, "carry." Every time I met someone new, I had to spell my name out, and if we had a new teacher I had to explain all over again that *I* was Rhys, a girl.

But by now I was used to my name and liked it. It sounded like wind over water or like fingers running all the way down a piano keyboard.

68

Grandma sorted through another pile of photos.

"All of these are my family. Left behind in Wales. Aunts, uncles, cousins." She passed the pictures to us one by one and the names slid together like a song: "Dillwen, Gwenno, Myvanwy, Blodwen, Prys, Marged, Rhonwen."

"I haven't seen these pictures in years," Mom commented.

Grandma handed me a cardboard folder. "This is your grandfather and me. Too bad you never knew him."

I looked at the faces, one clear-eyed and stern as if he bore all the problems of the world and the other, my grandmother, reflecting a world full of joy.

"I never looked like either one of you, did I?" Mom leaned over my shoulder, her cheek close to mine. "Funny how the family resemblance skipped to Rhys."

"You favor your father, whether you know it or not," Grandma said, quickly choosing another folder of pictures. "Why, Eve. Here are your high school graduation pictures. And your wedding pictures."

"My wedding pictures! I didn't know you saved them," Mom said in a small voice.

I met plenty of Rhyses that afternoon—all dead of course, but somehow, with Grandma's comments, alive.

Lew came later.

I was taking a shower and didn't hear him arrive, but when I ran down the stairs and glanced out the window, there were Mom and Lew at the end of the dock, Mom pointing at something across the lake.

My first thought was no wonder she was so pushy about taking her shower first. She knew he was coming.

And she must have known exactly when he got off work She was wearing a filmy blue peasant blouse with matching shorts. I had always realized she was quite attractive, but not quite *that* attractive.

If Mom had been June Rose Cronk on the third grade playground, I'd have tripped her so she got gravel in her knees and sand up her nose and grass stains on her dress. But this was no playground and she wasn't June Rose. She was my mother. That made it all worse.

So I did the only other thing I could think of. I ran back upstairs, tore off my shorts and t-shirt and slipped into my new red bikini that had taken me three months of coaxing to convince Mom I should have. Kim said it looked like two postage stamps and a Bandaid. I also pulled on a robe. After all, I had to get past Grandma. I needn't have worried. She was in the bathroom and I made it to the back door.

Mom and Lew didn't hear the door close. That's how wrapped up in each other they were. Halfway across the lawn, I pulled off my robe and draped it casually, I hoped, over my shoulder. They didn't notice me until I stepped on the dock. They turned, both laughing. I could have shoved them into the lake.

"Rhys!" they both said at once. Mom sounded as if someone had dropped an ice cube down her back, and Lew sounded just the way I hoped he would.

"Oh, hi," I said. "I hope I'm not interrupting anything."

I decided at this rate, it wouldn't take me long to become an accomplished liar. I wanted to interrupt! Better yet, I wanted to stop something before it started or maybe I wanted to start something before it could be stopped.

70

Either way, I didn't want to share Lew with my mother.

"Rhys." Mom put her hand on my shoulder and turned me around. "I still think I'd like that suit better in blue. It wouldn't be quite so . . . so . . . garish."

Lew didn't say anything.

I smiled at them both and walked to the end of the dock.

I heard Grandma calling from the porch. "Lew. Time to get back to work. There's one more box up here. And would you mind getting out the lawn mower when you're through?"

I carefully spread out my robe on the dock, lay down, and closed my eyes. I had never tried to foul up Mom when some man was interested in her. Of course, they were all so old and dull, they certainly didn't interest me anyway. She must have thought so too because she had never gone out with any of them more than two or three times, but this was different. This was *me*. And this was the most important thing that could ever happen. This wasn't Kim. And this was no dream. Lew was real. And he was mine. At least I wanted him to be.

It was hot on the dock and the wood burned my back through the robe. The gnats kept flying around my face and legs and arms. I couldn't go back up to the house so soon. I couldn't go swimming. I'd just washed my hair. I gritted my teeth and turned over on my stomach. Why, I wondered, for the first time . . . why couldn't Mom be ugly like June Rose Cronk's mother? Or stupid? Or grow warts? Or anything that would make Lew stop looking at her.

I stayed on the dock until I heard Lew start up the lawn mower. Grandma sat in a lawn chair, her eyes following Lew as if she were watching a tennis match.

71

"I don't like fringes around the edges," she called. "And be careful. Remember what you did to my rosemary."

I decided I wasn't going to have a chance to talk to Lew, so I picked up my robe and walked as slowly as I could toward the house. I timed it right, for I met Lew at the back steps. He stopped the mower for a minute, looked me over and grinned. "I think your mother's wrong."

"What do you mean?" I asked.

"The red's just fine. And don't forget, golf in the morning."

As if I could.

When I came up the porch steps, Mom was standing just inside the door, one hand on her hip, jaw set. "Rhys. I want to talk to you."

"Right now?" I pulled the robe around me. I already knew what she was going to say: that Lew was too old for me and that I was acting like a child. And I already knew what I was going to say to her: that she was too old for Lew and that she was acting like a juvenile.

"Right now," she said firmly. "It's about Grandma."

"What about Grandma?" I asked surprised. Mom had done it to me again. How many times before had she caught me off balance like that? Like the time she caught Kim and me trying to smoke her cigarettes. We'd expected a lecture, but instead she'd ignored the whole thing and suggested we all go down to the drive-in for a snack. For some reason, Kim and I never tried cigarettes again.

"We've got to do something." She waved her hand toward the left-over boxes piled against the walls and under the windows of the porch. "How can I tell her she will have to go back to the home?"

It's funny about feelings. I was all set to be angry and defensive about Lew, but now that we were going to talk about Grandma, all the bad feelings drained away. Mom wasn't even thinking of Lew.

"Why does she have to go back to the home? Why can't she stay here by herself? She gets around all right now."

"You don't understand. She could fall again. She's not capable of taking care of herself. I talked to Dave this afternoon. The people at the nursing home are quite sure there'll be a room opening up sometime the middle of next week."

"But if Grandma doesn't want to go back, you can't make her, can you? You can't commit people to a home."

"Of course not. But we've got to make her understand. We must remind her how different the house will be when we're gone. I've tried to talk to her, but she won't listen. She just changes the subject." Mom turned away. "You have time alone with her. Couldn't you broach the subject, in a roundabout way . . . and at least get her to talk about it?"

"Why me?"

"Because you're her granddaughter."

"That's a reason?" I asked, and I wasn't being smart.

"There's a special bond between grandmothers and granddaughters. It's different from any other. Maybe because there are no responsibilities."

I wasn't sure whether Mom was rationalizing or if she were right, but I did know she was worried.

"Okay. I'll try. But I don't think it'll work."

"You'll have to do it soon. We can't let her go on tearing up the house this way."

"Why not Virene? Why can't she talk to her?"

"She couldn't do that." Mother looked at me in amazement. "Virene's her friend."

I'm not sure Mother understood what she had just said.

8

Taken for a Ride

"Rhys. We seem to have the rest of the day to ourselves." Grandma watched me put my bicycle away. I had played golf with Lew every morning that week, but this was a Friday, his day off, so I had played only nine holes . . . alone.

"I thought first we could—"

Not the porch windows again, I hoped. Something from the basement? A letter to mail? A book from the library?

"Sure, what do you want me to do?"

"I didn't say you. I said *we*. Dust is piling up."

"But we just cleaned yesterday."

"Not in the house, Rhys. In my head. It's time for a good airing out. You'll want a shower. And why don't you put on those yellow slacks and that lovely blue shirt."

"What are we going to do?"

"We're going for a ride. After lunch."

"But I don't have my license yet. I can't drive."

"I can."

Something about the way she said it made me believe she could.

"I want to tie up a few loose ends."

I didn't ask where we were going.

It was one of those perfect days that happen at the end of June—bright and blue and beautiful as if the whole world were holding its breath before summer exploded. Mom had driven in to the library at Cummings, the only big city within seventy miles.

"Your mother is gone for the day. Lew went with her, you know."

I didn't know. He hadn't said anything to me and neither had Mom. I wondered when she'd asked him. Probably that bikini afternoon. No wonder I didn't get the why-don't-you-grow-up lecture that day. Just when I was beginning to get really mad, I decided that the reason Lew hadn't mentioned it to me was that it wasn't that important to him. Then, on the other hand, maybe Mom had set the whole thing up so that I'd have plenty of time with Grandma to "broach the subject in a round-about way."

"How come she asked Lew to go along with her?" I blurted out.

Grandma looked at me, her eyes kind. "He asked *her*, Rhys."

"But they don't even know each other . . ." I knew I was sounding like a child.

"Oh, I think they do, Rhys. But maybe your mother wanted to give us a day alone together." For a minute I wondered if it was true.

When did Lew have time to see Mom? Maybe on Fridays. Maybe Fridays were Eve days for him. Or maybe when he drove into town to pick up the mail. I could believe Mom, now, that coming back to Preston made her feel like a girl again. You would think an intelligent person would stop being a girl when she became a mother.

By the time we had finished lunch, and I had washed the dishes and got dressed, Grandma had her car backed out in the drive and was waiting behind the steering wheel. I must have looked a little worried.

"I've been driving for sixty years and never had an accident. Don't look so scared."

"But Mom. She'll . . ."

"What about your mother?"

"She'll die."

"I doubt it. You don't die from surprise. Besides, she doesn't need to know. You *can* keep a secret, can't you, Rhys?"

I thought about all the other secrets that were being kept that summer and climbed into the seat beside her.

"I want to drive around town again," Grandma explained as she backed the car, quite expertly, into the street. "You know, I'm safer driving a car than I am walking."

Grandma turned left onto Maple Avenue. "Now that house on your right, that was the old Armstrong place. Armstrongs started this town. Lovely woman, Mrs. Armstrong. I'd never have survived childhood if it hadn't been for her. And there on your left, back there behind that wrought-iron fence—can you see it back there? That belonged to your grandfather's people. It's a funeral home now."

We drove up and down the streets, with Grandma telling me the history of almost every house and business.

"That's the Blackburn house. Isn't that fussy? Money and no taste. My mother would have said they lacked breeding."

We finally finished the town and started around the lake road.

"That's Cottonwood Point there. Used to be covered with trees and in early summer the cotton fluff was like snow. Beautiful it was. And that's Shotgun Hill."

"They hunt there?"

Grandma chuckled. "Not exactly, but it was the start of a lot of quick marriages."

We saw Sutherland Beach, East End, Catfish Cove, Albertson's Inlet and . . . Grandma's Park.

"What about Grandpa? How come his name isn't on it?"

"It wasn't his land. It was mine. And I'm Wyn Rhys. After he died, I started using my own name again. I always did like the sound of it. It's easy to say. All you have to do is breathe out. Rhys."

Just when I thought we were going to start home, Grandma turned off the lake road and headed out toward the country.

"This road we're on—we're exactly five-and-a-half miles from town. That big walnut tree over on the right is where I found your mother one day, when she was only seven. You see, your grandfather had been elected mayor and the newspaper wanted a picture of the family. Well, I rounded up David, but I couldn't find your mother anywhere."

The car hit some loose gravel, but Grandma maneuvered it back onto the hard-packed track. "Eve had a bad habit of disappearing and not answering when I called. So this time she missed getting her picture taken. When she found out, she didn't say a word. Just marched off to her room and slammed the door. We didn't look for her until supper time. Some of her clothes were gone and so was her bicycle. We all went out in different directions looking for her. I found her there. Under that tree. Clothes on the ground. Standing beside her bicycle, crying."

"Scared?"

"Not Eve. Mad. Mad because she couldn't keep her clothes in the bicycle basket. I always understood David. but Eve was different." Grandma stepped down on the accelerator. "I never understood my daughter."

We turned around in a farmer's drive and headed back toward town in silence.

As we approached a crossroad, she slowed down. "Would you mind going to the cemetery with me? It's right along here."

"Do you want to?"

Grandma turned and looked at me. "Not so much want to. Think I should. I told you there were loose ends."

I began to wish that I had never promised Mom that I'd talk with Grandma about the nursing home. It wouldn't be so bad, I thought, if I could figure out how to begin, but I didn't think a cemetery was the right place.

We drove through a grove of oak trees nestled in a series of ravines. Grandma guided the car down the narrow dirt road, turned sharply toward the left, and stopped.

"I'll have to have my cane, Rhys. Will you get it from the back seat?"

Together we walked slowly across the new-mown grass to a marble headstone marked *Roberts*.

"Over there are the Rhyses. My mother and father. Brother Evan. Brother George." She pointed with her cane. "Sister Mary. And these are the Robertses."

I looked down at the stone. Under my grandfather's name were the dates of his birth and death and beside his name was "Wyn Rhys Roberts," the birth date carved, the death date a shiny blank.

"We agreed when we got married," Grandma frowned, "that we would hyphenate our names. Make it Rhys-Roberts. I always signed my name that way. He didn't, you see."

"You could get someone to come and put the hyphen in, couldn't you?" I suggested.

"No need to. I'm not going to be buried here anyway." She touched the stone with her cane. "It's one of the few times I ever lied to him."

"What do you mean?"

"Oh, your grandfather insisted on buying this fancy marker and having it ready for us. Made me promise I'd be buried beside him."

Mom wouldn't have liked what we were talking about.

"Eve and David don't know it yet, but I'm willing my body to the University Medical School. Lew's getting the papers for me. And I want you to make sure my instructions are followed."

"Why me?"

"Because you're my granddaughter."

"Oh, Grandma. We don't have to think about that now."

Grandma stood up straighter, barely resting her weight on her cane. "Anyone who lives must think of dying."

"But, Grandma . . ."

"Would you mind calling me Wyn? It would help me feel more like a person . . . again."

We left the cemetery, but we didn't turn back onto the lake road. Instead we drove north, past town.

I checked my watch.

"Don't you think we'd better start home? Mom and Lew should be back." I hated linking their names. It made him sound like my father.

I was sure if Mom found out what we'd been doing, she might not die, but she'd kill *me*.

"Oh, I forgot to tell you. When they left, Eve and Lew said they planned to stay in for dinner. It's good for your mother to get out for a change."

I looked out the side window. That's just what I wished . . . that Mom would get out. Get out from between Lew and me. Dinner? He hadn't even bought me a Coke at the pro shop.

"Aren't you tired?" I asked. Usually Grandma took a nap in the afternoon.

"Of course I'm tired, and I'm hungry too. That's why we're going to have dinner before we go home."

I was going to have dinner after all . . . with Grandma. Big deal!

She pulled into a half-filled parking lot. No pickups, I noticed, but large expensive cars instead.

The building looked like something from the cover of a gothic novel. It was a house, or maybe a mansion —three stories tall with a huge front door and round towers on either corner. And there were gaslights already flickering on the front lawn even though the sun hadn't set.

"Are you sure this is a place to eat?" I asked. "There isn't any sign."

"Of course it's a restaurant. Colby House. Been here for years. And we have reservations."

She was tired, I could see. "Would you like your cane?"

"I *never* like my cane. Now come along."

Tired or not, she walked, not like Twtty Wyn Hec, but like a queen, up the steps. I opened the heavy doors and followed her inside.

"Wyn. Wyn Rhys." The man's voice welcomed us. He moved out from something that looked like the kind of little podium a minister preaches from.

"Hello, Tim. This is my granddaughter Rhys. Rhys, Tim Colby."

I smiled at him and shook his hand, and while they talked, I looked around.

There were candles and mirrors and flowers everywhere and lots of antique furniture. Beside us, rising from the entrance, wound a heavy wooden staircase. From the room ahead I could hear voices and the clinking of silverware against china. And music. Some kind of string trio.

It was as if I'd stepped into a whole different world. I mean Mom and I had been in some very nice places to eat at home, but I hadn't expected a restaurant like this here. I wondered where Mom and Lew were.

"Let me show you to your table." The man gestured toward the next room.

We followed him.

"This is the table you wanted, isn't it, Wyn?"

"Yes, thank you," Grandma said. "I want to be near the music."

Grandma ordered a light meal for herself and a full dinner for me. This had to be the time, I decided, to mention the nursing home. The day had somehow funnelled itself so there was no escape that I could see. If I could just think of an opening sentence.

Grandma sat looking at me as if she were memorizing my face. "What are you thinking about, Rhys? You look so serious."

"Well," I began slowly. "I guess I—about this summer."

"So was I. Isn't that strange?" She fingered the corner of her napkin. "Has it been so bad? Here with me?" she asked, not looking directly at me. "In a way, you might feel I used you."

"But I understand," I said. "You didn't like it where you were. At Sunset Haven."

I was saying exactly the opposite of what I should have been saying.

"I knew you understood. I'm not sure your mother or your uncle do."

"But, Wyn . . . they only want what's best for you."

"No. They want what they *think* is best for me. There's something they don't know."

I can't explain, but I *felt* what I was going to hear before I knew what she was going to say.

"Rhys." She leaned back in her chair and put her hands palms down on the table. Her eyes reflected the candlelight. "I'm dying."

I heard the words but they were meaningless. In the midst of the music, the soft hum of people's voices, the polite clatter of silver on china, time stopped.

"I haven't told anyone." Her voice was even and quiet as if she had merely said, "Please pass the butter." She sipped her coffee. "I don't have much time left."

I thought of Mom . . . of Uncle Dave . . . of plans for the nursing home.

"And I intend to die in my own home." Her voice was steady.

The waitress appeared with our check, all smiles. "Did you enjoy your dinner?"

Grandma smiled back. "Immensely. Just leave the check, please." She was still smiling as the waitress left.

"Are you sure, Grandma?"

Her words had become real.

"I'm sure. There's no mistake."

"But why doesn't Mom know—or Uncle Dave?"

"Because I told the doctor not to tell them. For once he listened to me. He should. I'm paying him."

"Aren't you going to tell Mom? Why are you telling me?"

"Because it was easier to tell you. There's something special between a grandmother and a granddaughter."

I still wasn't sure what "special" meant, but it was a familiar line.

"Do you know how long? How long it will be?"

"Six months they said. Less, I think."

I tried not to count the months that were left. "Isn't there something they can do? Medicine? Operation? Something?"

"No. The most they can do is to provide a little pause. I've always hated pauses. Waiting for trains, buses, airplanes." She pulled crisp green bills from her purse and placed them on the check.

I didn't know what to do or what to say. Anything I

thought of seemed wrong. The only thing good was that I'd never managed to talk about her going back to the nursing home.

Grandma reached over and touched my arm softly.

"This wasn't fair either, was it? I didn't know how else to do it. But you're young. You're strong. And you can help me."

"What about Mom?"

"That's the other thing you and I have to settle."

"Grandma," I asked as we walked back to the car. "Would you like me to drive?"

"You don't have your license. I told you before I drive better than I walk. Besides I always finish what I start."

We drove home slowly, the sun low behind us.

"Now, about your mother. Could you tell her? Sort of broach the subject. In a roundabout way?"

"Oh Grandma . . . Wyn."

"Break it to her gently."

"Gently! How?"

"I don't know. I've tried to bring it up. She changes the subject. And I'm tired of pretending everything's all right."

I felt like a double agent. I stared into the growing shadows.

"When did you find out?" I finally managed.

"About a week before I fell and broke my hip."

"Why didn't you tell Mom then? Or Uncle Dave?"

"Because I had to come to terms with it myself, first. That's one good thing about a nursing home. It's a vacuum of time. There's nothing to do but think. I did a great deal of that."

I couldn't understand why I wasn't crying or at least

saying something to show Grandma that her sickness mattered. But she was sitting beside me, alive, guiding the car effortlessly.

"Haven't you told anyone?"

"Just my minister."

We turned onto the highway.

"Does it hurt?" Saying *it* made talking easier.

"No. Very little pain. But it's always there, waiting. I've learned to live with it finally. You can't wait too long to tell your mother. You're going home next week."

"I guess so." I barely spoke the words aloud.

The tires hummed monotonously. I glanced at the strong hand, stubby fingers curled around the steering wheel, coarse veins and tendons running up to bumps of knuckles.

I remembered how big and warm her hands had felt when I was little and she took me for a walk down by the lake. "Walk on the grass, Rhys Ann. You'll be safe. The Fairies of the Lake can't steal you if you can lay hold of a blade of grass."

I never played on the rocks down near the lake at Grandma's house. I always stayed within reach of a blade of grass . . . or her hand.

Mom's car was parked in front of the house when we got home, and she stood in the doorway.

"We misjudged our time. I thought we'd get home before they did," Grandma whispered as I helped her from the car. "We're in for it now. We don't have to tell how far we went."

"Mother!" Mom's voice was grim. "And you, Rhys!" Her voice was even grimmer. "I've been worried sick. Where have you been?"

"Out." Grandma let go of my arm and moved past Mom, down the hall. I followed.

"Did you and Lew have a nice dinner?" Grandma called back.

"Dinner! Who could think of dinner? I phoned earlier this afternoon to see if everything was all right and there was no answer. I kept calling. Still no answer, so we rushed home. I almost called the police. Where have you been?"

So they hadn't had dinner together, after all.

"Grandma took me for a ride," I said innocently.

Grandma chuckled. "That's one way to put it."

"How could you two have been so thoughtless? And you drove, Mother? You could have had an accident." Mom sounded as if she were scolding a naughty child.

"Grandma's a very good driver." I argued as if I were protecting a younger sister.

"But something might have happened," Mom went on.

"Something did happen," Grandma said, settling in her chair on the back porch. "We drove out to five-mile corner, to the cemetery, and then we ate at the Colby House."

"What on earth for?" Mom did not sit down in the chair Grandma indicated. "I would have taken you . . . if you'd asked."

"I didn't want to be taken. After all, you're leaving next week, aren't you? I'm going to be taking care of myself then."

I avoided looking at Mom.

"That's different. We're here now. And I'm responsible." Mom was talking too fast. "And Dave says—" She broke off.

"David doesn't know everything—even if he is a lawyer." Grandma slipped off her shoes. "You and David can't live my life for me or"—she stopped as if searching for a right word—"or . . . control my . . . my future."

I hoped Grandma would go on, but she didn't. What was wrong? Here were two grown women, tiptoeing around the truth. Why couldn't they talk to each other? They'd inch up to the edge and then back away.

"Mother, we have enough trouble living our own lives. We certainly don't want to interfere with yours." Mom's voice was getting higher. "We're just trying to do what's right."

Grandma's voice matched hers. "Then stop treating me as if I'm your child!"

"What am I doing that upsets you? I thought you wanted me here."

"Of course I want you here. But I didn't *need* you here." Grandma's voice dropped to a fierce whisper. "There's a difference, and you've never learned."

I couldn't stand it any longer. I was tired of being the only one who knew the truth. How did everything get to be my responsibility? Both of them had lived life-times longer than I. Hadn't they learned anything? Even to trust each other?

I jumped up from the couch.

"Dammit!" I shouted. "What's the matter with you two?"

They turned toward me in shocked silence.

"Grandma." I bent over her chair. "Your children want me to talk you into going back to Sunset Haven when we leave. They have a room already reserved for you."

I spun around and faced my mother. "And Mom . . ."

I took a deep breath. "Your mother wants me to tell you she is dying. Now are you both satisfied?"

I didn't wait for answers. I ran from the porch, up the stairs, and slammed my bedroom door behind me.

9

Plans

My alarm went off the next morning at the usual six o'clock. Lew was expecting me. I jumped out of bed, headed toward the shower and stopped. My feet didn't move. Lew had spent all yesterday with Mom, and he hadn't told me he was going. They had even been going to have dinner together. Of course they didn't, but that wasn't the point. They were planning on it.

There had been many mornings when I had sat and waited for him. This morning he could wait for me . . . all morning. I turned and headed back to bed. I pulled the covers over my head and tried to go back to sleep. It didn't work. Once you start thinking, it's impossible to stop. My mind was tugged two ways. After last night, I didn't want to face Mom and Grandma. And after yesterday, I didn't want to see Lew. I did, of course, but more than that I wanted him to *miss* me.

Then I began to wonder if he ever wanted to be with me as much as I wanted to be with him. The wanting was something I had never felt before. It wasn't the doing things with him like playing golf and talking and laughing; it was just the being with him that felt so right.

I turned over on my stomach and buried my face in the pillow. Why Lew? Why Lew and not Kim? Why now with time running out . . . when there was only a week or so left? Why couldn't I have been born eight or nine years earlier? Or Lew eight or nine years later. And what was there about him that was so different, that made me feel more alive than I had ever been? That could make me almost hate my own mother? At the beginning of the summer, it was all so simple. Everything was separate: Grandma, Mom, Virene, Lew, me. Now all of us were tangled together and I wasn't sure what I felt about any of them . . . except Lew.

I heard Mom in the shower, but I did not move. I must have fallen asleep, for when I woke, the sun glinting across the lake was so brilliant that I could no longer sleep or pretend to.

Mom's library books were still stacked on the table at the bottom of the stairs. I heard voices from the kitchen.

"It needs more water, Eve. Wyn likes it thin." It was Virene, and I was glad. With Vi around we wouldn't have to talk, and it would be easier for us all to pretend that nothing had happened.

"Rhys." Virene said, looking up from the stove where she was stirring something. "I thought you played golf with Lew every morning."

"Not today."

"What's happening around here? Wyn sleeping late. Eve making oatmeal, and you here for breakfast."

"Change doesn't hurt anyone," Mom answered without looking up from sprinkling raisins into the saucepan.

"Does Wyn feel all right?" Virene asked.

"She's fine," Mom answered. "She stayed up a little past her bedtime last night. That's all."

"I didn't even hear you come to bed, Mom," I inserted, attempting to be casual.

"It was late," Mom answered without looking at me.

"Say, Eve." Virene lowered herself into a chair. "What's all this clear-out-the-attic business? Is she going to have an auction after all?"

"No. She's just going through her things. Do you want some oatmeal, Rhys?"

"Do I have a choice?"

"No."

"Then I'll have some oatmeal."

The whole question and answer was a little set pattern that Mom and I always went through. It had been funny to us once. It was not funny this morning.

"Vi, do you want some?"

"Never touch it, Eve. Say, how much longer do you two plan to be here?"

Mom dipped my oatmeal into a bowl. "I haven't had a chance to talk to Rhys yet, but another month . . . or two. Would that be all right, Rhys?"

A month or two! The rest of the summer . . . with Lew. Time! More time for us. Thirty days. Sixty days even.

I took a bite of oatmeal. It was soft and warm against my tongue. We would have time for long walks, picnics, golf before breakfast.

"I guess it's all right with me," I answered without looking up.

It became so quiet in the kitchen, I realized I should be saying something more. I choked out a smile. "Maybe I'll enter the Ladies' Open, then. Lew thinks I'd have a good chance to win."

Lew had never mentioned the meet. I'd seen the entry form posted in the pro shop.

"But, Mom. What about your dissertation?" At least that part wasn't a lie.

"I'll call my professor today. I'm sure we can take care of everything by mail. That'll be no problem."

"You know,"—Virene leaned her elbows on the table —"it was the best medicine in the world for Wynnie, getting her out of that nursing home and being in her own home again."

I was so excited about staying that I'd forgotten for a moment *why* we were staying.

"Imagine David was a little upset, wasn't he?" Virene went on.

"We all were—at first," Mom said with a quick glance at me.

"You know she won't go back there, don't you?"

"I know," Mom said softly.

"You don't need to worry. I'll keep a close eye on her. I have an ex-daughter-in-law who's a licensed nurse. I could get her. Wyn'll be all right."

"When did she tell you?" I asked, sure that Virene knew all about Grandma.

"She didn't. We haven't been friends for forty years for nothing. Some things we don't have to put into words. She's been failing for the last year. I could see it. Many's the time she was on the verge of telling me, but she never could. It's in her lungs, isn't it? My first husband's mother acted the same way."

I looked up. Grandma was standing in the doorway. "I suppose you've been discussing me?"

Virene turned. Her voice softened. "Wynnie! Of course we have. Who else is worth talking about?"

It was as if Virene had said, "I love you."

Before Mom could dish up her own oatmeal, the phone rang. It was Lew. I thought she would call me to the phone, but she didn't.

"No, no. Everything's all right. They got back shortly after I arrived. They went out to dinner. Dinner, yes. Oh. She slept late this morning. . . ."

She was *me*. Why didn't he ask to talk to me?

"No. Nothing's wrong. Just a change in plans. We may stay the rest of the summer."

I wanted to tell him.

"Oh, all right. I'll tell her. Yes. And so nice of you to call."

Mom came through the kitchen door. "That was Lew. He wanted to make sure everything was all right." She stopped and poured herself a cup of coffee. "I told him the two of you had gone out for dinner and of our change of plans."

I clenched my fists under the table.

"Oh, by the way, Rhys." She sipped her coffee, both elbows on the table. "If you're interested in playing golf this evening, he said he'd stop by and pick you up around six. You don't need to call him back, unless you don't want to go."

I sneaked a look at my watch. Eight more hours. And a month or more of time.

Later that day, while Grandma was napping, Mom put in a call to Uncle Dave. "I'm not asking you, Dave.

This time I'm telling you. We're not putting Mother back in the home. I've already cancelled her room. We're staying."

There was a space of minutes when Mom did not say anything; then she broke in. "How long? As long as it takes."

After she hung up, she turned to me. "Is that all right with you, Rhys? It might mean a semester's leave of absence for me. And going to school here for you."

"I don't care," I said. "One thing for sure. I won't have to sit through Bugs Mason's biology class."

I didn't wait for her answer because I heard Lew's car in the drive. I was in the car before Lew had a chance to get out.

"What's up? Someone chasing you?"

"Yes, and I don't intend to be cut off at the pass."

He shoved the car into reverse and we spun out into the street and headed in the opposite direction from the country club.

"Aren't we going to play golf?"

"Who wants to play golf?"

"Not me. I didn't even bring my golf shoes. Then where are we going?"

"I was cheated out of dinner last night, thanks to you. Now you're going to pay for it."

Several lovely ideas of payment floated through my mind. I was glad I had worn my best slacks. Mom hadn't even noticed.

For a while, we drove without talking. I looked at his hands on the steering wheel. They were just as beautiful as his teeth. I wondered why Kim and I had never thought of hands. I'd have to tell him when I got home. Or maybe I wouldn't. There were some things he'd have to find out for himself.

Just when I was reminding myself that I should be angry with Lew about going off with Mom and not saying anything, he turned to me and smiled.

I never knew that I could feel someone else's smile all the way inside.

I smiled back. He reached over and for a second, very softly, touched the back of my hand.

"You know," he said, "I'm glad there's a Rhys."

I was too, and then I wondered if he had said, "I'm glad there's an Eve." Could he have two scripts: one for me and one for Mom? It might be like instant replay.

The feeling was heightened when we turned into the drive of the Colby House.

"Why here?" I asked.

"I said we were going to have dinner and this is the best place around."

"Rhys," Mr. Colby said, stepping out from behind the same little podium.

"You remember my name?"

"I'd remember you any time."

Lew looked down at me, one eyebrow raised. "You've been here before?"

I swallowed. "Yeah. Last night."

"Is this all right?" Mr. Colby led us to a table.

It was. It was perfect: across the room from where Grandma and I had sat. We were in a dimly-lit corner, the music behind us. Everything was the same, yet everything was different. The precisely folded napkin, the single carnation in the cut glass vase, the sparkling silver, even the ash tray with the embossed match folder—all prepared and waiting for Lew and me.

96

"Would you like a drink before dinner?" Lew asked.

Just when I was feeling completely adult, he had asked me the impossible question. I'd have to tell him that I was too young.

"Or wine with dinner?"

"Wine with dinner," I sighed with relief.

Lew ordered for both of us. I don't remember what we ate. We talked. I don't remember what we talked about. I was aware only of candlelight and velvet music.

The waitress came with coffee in shell-thin demitasse cups.

"Your mother said you're staying on."

"Yes, yes, we are." I felt my smile widen, then disappear.

He leaned toward me. "Is something wrong?"

"I don't know, really." I folded my napkin carefully. "Can something be right and wrong at the same time?"

"That's what I've been wondering. I think so."

"The reason we're staying . . ." I turned and looked across at the table where Grandma and I had sat the night before. "Grandma's dying. She told me last night. Here. At dinner."

"Then it is true. Virene was right. And there's nothing you can do, is there?"

"Be here, I guess. And wait. But, Lew . . ." I didn't know how to go on. I still wasn't sure of all the things I was feeling, but maybe if I talked to him, put the confusion into words, maybe I'd be able to sort things out.

"Wait," he said. "Let's get out of here first."

We drove slowly down a one-lane, rutted dirt road, tree limbs scratching against the side of the car.

"This is the game reserve. You remember the herons

we saw? They nest back in here, and this time of evening we should be able to see deer."

He pulled off the road under some trees. He turned toward me, leaned back against the door and said, "Okay. Now tell me about it."

And so I told him how glad I was that we were staying . . . because of him. Why I felt guilty about being so glad because of Grandma, how each day more with him was one day less of Grandma's life and it was like trying to add and subtract at the same time.

He didn't move to touch me; he sat and watched as if the sight of me filled his eyes.

I stopped talking. I was suddenly very tired.

"You asked," he began, "if something could be right and wrong at the same time. I understand. It's what I've been feeling about you. Look, Rhys, I'm twenty-six and you're only eighteen."

At first I was stunned. Then I felt my head moving slowly from side to side.

"I am, Rhys. Maybe I look younger, but I'm eight years older than you."

"Oh, you're wrong! Maybe I should have told you, but I thought you knew. I'm sixteen."

"Oh, my god," he said. "You're illegal." Then he started to laugh.

It wasn't really funny, but I laughed too, and all of a sudden it was just like it had been on the playground merry-go-round, and what should have been a tender, romantic moment turned into a beautiful joke.

But when we kissed, it was not funny at all.

And it wasn't very funny four hours later when I walked into the house and found Mom waiting for me.

"Do you know what time it is?"

"No," I said, tucking my shirt into my slacks. "I didn't bother to wear my watch."

"I think we'd better have a little talk. Your grandmother's sleeping. Come upstairs."

I followed reluctantly. Any little talks with Mom were never little when she used that tone. I opened the door to my room and flipped on the light. If we were going to talk it was going to be in *my* territory. Just like golf, you have an advantage on your home course.

"Well, what do you want to talk about?" I kicked off my sandals and sprawled across the bed.

"It's one-thirty in the morning and don't tell me you've been playing golf. In sandals."

"I wasn't. Lew took me out to dinner." I tried to keep the triumph out of my voice.

"Nobody eats dinner for seven and a half hours."

"Depends on how hungry you are, I suppose." It was the wrong thing for me to say.

Mom didn't answer. She pulled up a chair and sat down and looked at me. "Rhys," she said, her voice too quiet. "What's going on? You're only sixteen."

"Well, I'm sure not forty-two." It was nasty, but I couldn't resist.

I really didn't like what was happening: the sound of our words, the roles we were playing, the coldness between us.

"I guess that wasn't very nice," I added. "To tell you the truth, we ate at the Colby House, drove around a while, went out to the game reserve, sat and talked and watched for deer and stuff like that."

She sat still for a minute, then got up and walked

slowly to the window. "You find him very attractive, don't you?"

"Don't you?"

I saw her back stiffen.

"Of course I do. But he's too young. And so are you."

"What's age got to do with it?" I realized what I had said and felt as if I had blown a one-foot putt on the last hole.

Mom half-turned and leaned against the window. "Maybe everything. Maybe nothing. I just don't want you to be hurt. I certainly don't want to be the one that hurts you, and I'm afraid I have. I didn't realize until tonight that it was happening. I don't love Lew. I just find his company charming and delightful, and obviously you do too." She ended with a half smile.

I knew she was being honest. I sat up, cross-legged on the bed, and hugged my pillow. "Oh, Mom," I said, trying to keep my voice from shaking. "Do you know I almost hated you?"

"He's that important to you?"

"Yes . . ." I hesitated and added the words I didn't want to say. "For right now, he is."

She walked slowly toward the door. "The first time a woman falls in love is the most beautiful and often the most painful. I told you that I didn't want to hurt you, and you know, somehow, I don't think Lew will either."

It was the most loving thing my mother had ever said to me.

10

Guests

"Wyn needs something to occupy her time," Virene announced one day as she was leaving. "She's turning into a zombie, sitting out there all day. Drying up like a weed."

"I know," Mom agreed. "She naps all day, and then wonders why she can't sleep at night. That porch is beginning to look like a ghetto, and she won't let me move a thing to clean."

"Except the windows!" I reminded them.

"Oh, yes. Her windows to the lake are always clean," Mom said.

"Cleaned by *me*," I quickly added.

"It's not good, her losing interest in everything this way. Eve, you should be able to suggest something."

"Let's not bother with the herb garden today." Grandma sighed when I came back from the golf course the next morning.

She was lying in the wicker chaise longue, her shoes

off, an empty glass on the table beside her along with a half-worked crossword puzzle from the morning paper, a partly-eaten apple and an unopened letter. She was still in her bathrobe, her hair uncombed, her eyes closed. I could see the outline of her skull beneath the white stretched skin.

I tossed my golf shoes in the corner. "What would you like to do?"

"Nothing."

Twtti Wyn Hec had flown. It was almost as if the rhyme had come true. Her secret had been discovered, and she was quitting.

I wondered if Grandma felt the way I sometimes did after I made the qualifying round for a golf tournament. You get yourself completely psyched up to make the cut, and if you do, even though you know the hardest part is coming, there's a kind of letdown, and for a while, you just don't care about anything. Could dying be as simple as playing a game?

"Why don't you finish your crossword puzzle? You told me once they hadn't made one you couldn't solve."

"I don't feel up to it." Her voice was listless.

"Could I get you some more tea? Or help you get dressed?"

"I don't feel like getting dressed."

"But Grandma, you haven't even opened your mail."

"I know. It's from Alice. She never says anything, anyway. But if you think you have to do something, you can read it to me."

"Who's Alice?"

"Alice was a dear old friend. Now she's just an old friend and not very dear."

I opened the letter and began to read.

102

My dearest Wyn,
I'm no good most days, but worse today so I thought
I'd write to you.

"See what I mean? What's dear about that?" Grandma
interrupted. "But go on. You might as well finish as long
as you started."

Guess I'm like that lady in the story. I get up in the
morning and read the death notices in the paper,
and if my name isn't there, I just eat breakfast and go
back to bed.

"Alice died years ago." Grandma snorted. "They just
haven't printed her obituary."
I jumped ahead in the letter. Certainly there had to be
something better. I skipped a paragraph and tried again.

Our hometown Margaret is in Mercy Hospital.
Think she is really in a bad way. They removed her
gall . . ."

I stopped and jumped ahead again.

Margaret Hill, our old next-door neighbor, is in the
Methodist Hospital with a blood clot in her . . .

It had to get better. I tried once more.

Mabel Daniels had colon surgery.

I mumbled my way through that.

All I hear from Martha Winslow is poor health. Gerald's sister is coming to visit. I'm not too eager about that. I can think of other things I'd rather do than entertain her. There was something else I meant to write you about, but it seems like these days I forget more than I remember.

I had come to the end. Written sideways up the margin of the page was "Sorry. I haven't left room on the page to say love, Alice."

I folded the page and slipped it back in the envelope. "It was a nice letter," I said.

Grandma opened her eyes and turned her head slowly to look at me. "Wasn't it though?" She carefully caught up a wisp of hair, tucked it neatly behind one ear, and folded her hands in her lap. "Dear, dear Alice," she breathed looking up at the ceiling. "Sending her ray of sunshine to brighten my corner."

She glanced over again at me and broke out into genuine Twtti Wyn Hec laughter.

When Grandma laughed, all of her laughed: eyes, mouth, cheeks, body.

"Oh my dear Rhys." She wiped the tears from her eyes. "It's good to be able to laugh. Cleans out the sinuses. Straightens out the kinks."

"You were getting a bit kinky, Grandma."

"My world's grown a bit kinky lately. But Alice's letter gave me an idea. I need to do something different. You know—I think I need to give a party."

"A party!"

We had never finished going through the attic boxes; in fact, they were scattered all over the house. We had never got to the basement, the porch was a ghetto, and Grandma a mess.

"When?"

"Next week, I think. You and Eve and Virene and I. We'll get this house cleaned up. I'll have Virene make an appointment for me to get my hair fixed. Think I'll have it cut."

"Who's coming?"

"I'll ask my friends from Wing Two out at Sunset Haven."

Mother greeted the news with a combination of pleasure and alarm. "It's a lovely idea, Mother, but are you sure you feel strong enough?"

Virene's reaction was more enthusiastic. "Best idea you've had in years. You were well on your way to becoming a dried old prune!"

Then the real planning began, the four of us sitting at the kitchen table while Grandma assigned duties.

"How many do you want to invite?" Mother was always the statistician.

"Hattie Daniels, of course. I hope she can stay awake. Little Nellie. She has a tendency to wander off. Dorothy. It'll give her a chance to wear her diamonds. Wanda. And if we have Wanda, we'll have to have Albert. They're engaged."

"Engaged!" I exclaimed.

"Certainly." Grandma's eyes bored through me. "Just because they're in a nursing home doesn't mean they can't be in love."

I avoided looking at Mom.

"They're hunting for an apartment," Grandma went on. "Albert can bring them over. He used to be an undertaker, so he has a big car with jump seats."

Grandma was alive again.

"What do you want to serve? Is this just for an afternoon or is it a luncheon?" Mom asked, jotting down items on Grandma's telephone pad.

"We're going to do it up right. Sweet rolls at ten. Rhys can help me bake them. Lunch around two. And homemade ice cream and cake at four."

"Are you thinking of a sit-down lunch, buffet, or what?" Mom was a stickler on organization.

"I'm not sure yet," Grandma replied. "I know what *not*. Not anything they get at the home."

"I know," Virene said, standing up suddenly and almost upsetting the table. "I'll have it brought down from the truck stop. Fried chicken, cheeseburgers, French fries, baked beans, cole slaw. Greasy, but good. Smorgasbord. Give them their choice, for a change."

Grandma beamed. "I think that's the best idea yet."

"Mother, do you still have that electric ice cream freezer we gave you for Christmas once?"

"It's down in the basement somewhere, I think."

"Don't bother digging it out," Virene said with a decisive wave. "We'll use my old hand crank. Tastes better. Got a good recipe for rum raisin. That'll perk up the party. Albert and I can take turns cranking."

"And the cake," Grandma hurried on. "I'll bake my extra rich double chocolate fudge."

"But, Grandma," I said. "Do you suppose they'll all be able to come?"

"Of course." Grandma winked at me. "Where else do they have to go?"

They came up the front walk, five of them, like a weary scout troop, Albert in the lead. He ushered them into the house as if he were supervising a memorial service.

"He was the friendliest undertaker in the county," Grandma had said.

"My dear Wyn. So nice of you to ask us." Dorothy had worn all her diamonds—in her ears, around her neck, on her wrists and fingers, and a large sunburst brooch on her dress.

"Isn't it lovely," breathed Hattie, her eyes slowly pulling her head from side to side.

Albert guided Wanda by the elbow. "You couldn't have picked a nicer day. Just right for an outing."

Wanda laughed happily.

Virene beckoned from the back porch. "Come on out. We've got it all set up out here."

They sat around the table that Vi had moved out from the kitchen and "oh-ed" and "ah-ed" over Grandma's sweet rolls and marveled at the blueness of the lake through the windows I had washed and polished that morning. Nellie spilled her coffee, but no one minded. Later Vi shooed them out on the back lawn with, "Go outside now. We have to use this table to get lunch."

Grandma whispered to me, "Rhys, keep an eye on Nellie. Sometimes she gets lost."

I stood at the porch window and watched them, a gray cluster admiring Grandma's rose garden. I don't know why, but they seemed grotesque to me—not because they were old, but more as if they had been put away someplace, like vegetables left too long in the bottom of a refrigerator. I could not imagine Lew and me ever looking like them. Grandma was the only one alive, standing in the middle, talking, laughing, gesturing.

"Eve," Vi said. "What do you say we take this stuff

out there and let them sit at the picnic table? That way they won't have to take on that step again."

Vi's truck-stop dinner was overwhelmingly successful. They ate everything, and Hattie did not fall asleep once.

They rested after lunch, in a circle of contented silence, until Vi came through the door, cradling the ice cream freezer and shouting, "Come on, Albert. Time for a little exercise."

"Would you like to cut some flowers to take home with you?" Mom suggested. "I've got scissors and some wrapping paper here. There's some mint down in the herb garden too."

That must have been when Nellie wandered off. No one noticed until the ice cream was ready.

"Rhys!" Grandma called. "Come here a minute. I think Nellie's gone. Will you go find her? She can't have strayed far."

I found Nellie down by the lake in the park playground. She was sitting in a swing, pushing herself with one foot.

"The ice cream is ready, now, Nellie," I said.

"I knew you'd come. Where are my other children? Do you think it's going to storm?"

"It's not going to storm. They're waiting for us. Come on, let's go find them." I took her hand and helped her from the swing. She did not let go of me as we walked back to the house, her hand fragile in mine.

Vi's rum-and-raisin ice cream was as much of a success as the dinner. There was hardly enough left for Mom and me.

The breeze off the lake turned cool.

"Should we go inside?" Grandma suggested.

"I think we'd better," Mom agreed, folding up her chair.

They left even more slowly than they had entered, Albert still in the lead. Nellie trailed behind, and when she passed me, she brushed the palm of her hand across my cheek and said, "Goodbye, Rhys."

We stood together at the front door, Grandma, Mom and I—Vi was in the kitchen "doing up" the dishes. Albert backed down the drive so slowly that twice the engine stalled.

"Well," Grandma turned and walked down the hall. "What do you think?"

Mom didn't answer, but I did.

"I'm glad you're home, Grandma."

11

The Party's Over

I tiptoed down the stairs the next morning, early—a little after five. I had decided to enter the Women's Open, and Lew had promised to help me with my long approaches if I'd get out to the course by six o'clock every morning. That way we'd still have time to play a round or two before he had to open up the shop.

I was beginning to feel a bit guilty about Kim. He had written three letters asking how things were going with Lew, and I hadn't answered any of them. I guess I didn't want to share Lew with anyone.

I was always careful not to disturb Grandma, but she claimed she always heard me leave anyway. I don't think she did, but this morning I discovered I'd left my golf shoes out on her porch.

I stepped carefully across the kitchen, trying to avoid the squeaky board by the refrigerator, knelt down in the doorway, and reached around the corner for my shoes.

The sun was casting shimmering spears across the lake; the lawn was still in shadow. I glanced over to see if Grandma had heard me. The bed was empty. The covers were not even disturbed.

Maybe she was sleeping on the couch in the front parlor. I walked down the hall, still holding my golf shoes. The parlor was empty. So was the living room.

She couldn't have gone upstairs to use one of the other bedrooms—or could she?

I ran up the stairs and looked into the rooms, one by one.

"What are you doing?" Mom stood in the door of her bedroom, blinking against the light.

"Grandma! She's gone!"

"She can't be."

"But she is."

"Oh my God." It sounded almost like a prayer. "Did you look in the basement?"

"No. I—"

Mom rushed past me. I followed. She yanked the basement door open and turned on the light. The basement was empty.

"Look and see if her car's in the garage. I'll get dressed."

The car was still in the garage. I circled the house, but there was no sign of Grandma.

Mom was just hanging up the phone when I came in. "I've called Virene. Mother's not there. Virene and Lew are going to take their cars to look for her. You and I can look along the lake."

"Mom, you don't think she would . . ." I stopped in the middle of the lawn and grabbed Mom's arm.

"It's possible. Anything's possible. You go down by the park. I'll go the other way."

We ran off in opposite directions. I tried not to think about the lake and Grandma's stories about water.

The park was empty and no one was sitting on the benches that edged the lake. Maybe Mom had found her. I turned and ran back to the house.

"No sign of her." Mom's face was pale. "There's Virene's car. Maybe we'd better call the police."

We burst through the porch door. Mom stopped and reached for my hand. Then I heard Grandma's voice from the kitchen.

"Haven't heard one in years, Vi."

The smell of coffee filled the air.

"Oh, Rhys." Mom pulled me close and rested her cheek against mine. "You just don't know."

I hugged her. "Oh, yes I do."

Virene and Grandma were sitting at the kitchen table. She looked up at us her face glowing. "I'm sorry that you were worried. If I'd known, I'd have left a note, but I couldn't sleep."

Mom sat down slowly. I leaned against the counter.

"It doesn't matter now, but where were you? Are you all right?"

"She's fine." Vi patted Grandma's hand. "She was here when I got to the house. Even had the coffee made."

Grandma reached across the table, smoothed my mother's hair, and smiled. "Don't worry. I wasn't running *from* anything, Eve. I was running toward . . ." She paused. "Well, not running. Walking."

"Toward what?" I asked.

"Toward some damn bird!" Virene said.

"I suppose it was around two in the morning. The

moon was very bright last night. Like magic. I heard an owl. I'm surprised it didn't wake you, it was so close. I was positive it was a horned owl. We haven't had them around here since I was a child!"

"And you had to follow it?" Mom squeezed Grandma's hand.

I had half-expected Mom to start scolding Grandma and for Grandma to be defensive. Instead I saw two people who cared about each other and who, for a moment at least, understood a lifetime of missed understanding.

"She's always had a thing for birds." Virene hunched over her coffee cup—a cigarette dangling from the corner of her mouth.

"It was in the pine tree, but when I went outside, it flew across the street. So I sat on the front porch until it got light enough to see. Then I walked across the street to Cora's back yard."

"And was it a horned owl?" I asked.

"Yes, it was a horned owl."

"You should write to the Audubon Society," Mom suggested.

"I may just do that."

The phone rang and while Mom went to answer it, I poured more coffee for Virene and Grandma.

"It's for you, Rhys." When Mom and I met in the doorway, she shrugged her shoulders and smiled. "It's Lew."

He told me he knew Grandma was okay, but he hoped Mom and I weren't upset. There was a funny kind of formality in his voice that made me uncomfortable. I had been hearing it ever since that night he had taken me out to dinner.

"Is anything wrong?" I asked.

"Of course not. Why?"

"I don't know. You just sound . . . funny."

"Must be this phone. And the shop's full of people."

"Oh," I said.

"I'll see you tomorrow."

"Yes," I said and hung up.

There was something wrong. I knew it. Was he bored with me already? What had I done wrong? Maybe I'd been too eager. Too easy. Too young. I couldn't talk to Mom, and Grandma would never understand. She was much too old. I went back into the kitchen, trying not to look at anyone. I needn't have bothered. Virene was talking.

"I'm going to take Wyn out to Gladys to tell her about the horned owl. Gladys is our bird person. She keeps track of all kinds of them, bands them, wraps little doo-dads around their legs, and all that crazy business."

"Now, Virene," Grandma protested. "It's not crazy business. It's a science. Gladys is an ornithologist."

"I don't care what she does in her spare time. She's for the birds as far as I'm concerned."

I looked at Mom. She shrugged again.

After Grandma and Virene left, Mom went up to her room to work and I was left alone downstairs in Grandma's house. I didn't feel like reading or listening to records. I guess I felt like thinking, so I curled up in Grandma's Queen Anne chair. You couldn't sit in Grandma's parlor without looking at her painting of the lake. It really was an interesting picture, if not remarkable. Of course, I was no art critic, but there was a sort of primitive rightness about it. It could just as easily have been a sunrise instead of a sunset, if you didn't know the direction. Except somehow it didn't look like a sunrise. It wasn't so much the color, but it just felt like an ending, not a beginning.

I heard a car in the drive. It was too soon for Grandma and Virene. Maybe it was Lew. I ran to the window and looked out. Vi was half carrying Grandma up the front steps.

"Mom!" I shouted. "It's Grandma. Something's wrong."

Mom rushed down the stairs just as I opened the front door.

"Now, now," Vi said, but her jaw was set. "Nothing to worry about. Wyn just needs to lie down."

Grandma sagged in the circle of Vi's big arm and tried to smile at us, but her face was pale and she wasn't breathing right.

"I think I'd better lie down for a little while," she said weakly. "Get me my herb tea, Rhys, from the refrigerator."

Together Mom and Vi got her to bed and by the time I brought the tea, Grandma's eyes were closed and she was breathing more regularly.

The three of us went back to the kitchen. "I think," Vi said, "you may want to call the doctor."

"What happened?" I asked.

"In the car. At the five-mile corner. I heard her gasp. I think she may have passed out for a minute or two. I wanted to take her straight to the doctor, but she wouldn't let me. Said she wasn't in any pain, but I wouldn't count on that."

Mother came back from the telephone. "He'll be right over. I told him it was an emergency."

115

It was an hour before he came. Grandma had not moved.

We sat huddled around the kitchen table, Vi and Mom and I, not looking at each other, Vi smoking and Mom too—in Grandma's house.

"I shouldn't have taken her, but she wanted to go."

"Oh, Vi," Mom said. "It's not your fault. The party and last night were too much for her."

"I don't know . . . why they bothered you," we heard Grandma say. "I'll be fine as soon as I catch my breath."

The doctor's voice was a low murmur and he talked for a long time.

"Should I call David, Vi?" Mom asked.

"Why don't we wait?" I said, surprising myself.

"Rhys is right," Vi assured us. "We'll see what the doctor has to say."

"No." Grandma's voice was clear and firm. "I told you that before, and I haven't changed my mind."

Vi winked at me. "She'll be all right. Stubborn old gal."

There was no answer to Grandma's remark. There was a long pause, and then the doctor appeared in the doorway.

"I've given her a sedative. She'll be asleep in a few minutes." He sat at the table with us. Vi made a half-hearted move to leave, but she stayed.

"There's no immediate cause for alarm," the doctor explained. "Things are moving faster than I anticipated. She'll be up again in a day or two. I tried to talk her into coming in to the hospital, but she refused."

"She'll keep on refusing, Doc, if I know her," Vi said.

The doctor smiled ruefully, "I know. She won't listen to me. But you—" He turned to Mom. "You're her daugh-

116

ter. I'm not concerned about her this time, but it's going to get worse very soon. Have you ever cared for a terminal patient?"

Mom shook her head slowly.

"It's an agonizing task, especially if the person is close to you. Now we have the facilities at the hospital to care for her. We might be able to prolong her life for months with our support systems."

"You mean prolong her death," Vi muttered.

The doctor looked embarrassed. "Virene, you do know how to put things in plain words."

"How soon?" Mom asked.

"Well, she's a remarkable woman. A month. Maybe less, maybe more. Frankly, at this stage, I think it depends upon what she wants."

"But she really doesn't look sick," I said.

The doctor frowned. "I know. That's the thing that makes it so hard. There's the weight loss, of course. She'll tire more readily. Her appetite will fail. And in the end, a respiratory or heart decline. We can control the pain."

He was talking about my grandmother, but he sounded as if he were quoting from a textbook.

"Eventually, and I have to be completely honest with you,"—he turned toward Mom—"it will mean total bed care. That means bedpans, baths, lifting, turning, changing bed linens, and finally twenty-four-hour attention."

Mom looked directly at me, asking with her eyes. I stopped thinking about Grandma. What if it had been Mom? I nodded.

"Are you sure you want to take care of her here?" the doctor asked again.

"Yes," Mom said.

The doctor left, convinced.

117

"Say," Vi said. "When it comes to it . . ." She stopped. For a minute I thought she was going to cry, but she didn't. She cleared her throat and went on. "There's a rental place over in Halifax—has hospital beds and all that stuff. When we need one, it won't be any trick at all to have it sent over."

"Let me jot down that name, Vi."

"Oh don't bother, Eve. I own it. Shrimp McKinley runs it. Shrimp was my first husband."

12

Choices

Reverend Baddeley came the first thing next morning.

"Bad news travels fast," Grandma called from her porch. "Who told you?"

He hurried down the hall. "Oh, I have my grapevine. Cora saw the doctor's car here yesterday afternoon."

"Rhys," Grandma said, gesturing toward the kitchen. "The usual for the Englishman."

"Wyn," he murmured. "Don't do this to me."

I didn't hear her answer as I moved toward the kitchen, but I knew he didn't mean the tea.

When I got back to the porch, Grandma looked up at me. "Would you water my herbs before it gets too hot? It shouldn't take more than half an hour."

I obediently disappeared.

I turned on the tap and adjusted the sprinklers so that the water fell in a soft, gentle arc. The morning sun caught the mist, turning it into a prism of color. I sat in the grass and listened to the splashing above the rise and fall of the two voices on the porch and the occasional laughter.

It sounds crazy, but sitting there, I started doing the same thing Grandma did—talking to the plants. I even remembered the names she called them and soon I was down on my knees pinching off dead leaves, loosening dirt around the stems, and pulling out an occasional weed. I wished I could have, as easily, pulled out the questions that were growing in my mind. Golf that morning with Lew had been strange, and I didn't know how or why. We laughed and talked the same way we always did, but something was missing. It was as if I could have been anybody, not someone special.

As I was readjusting the sprinkler I glanced up toward the porch. At first I thought something was wrong, because Reverend Baddeley was standing, holding my grandmother in his arms. I almost started to run across the lawn; then I saw her cradle his face in both her hands. I looked away as embarrassed as if I had overheard a conversation. When I looked again, they were sitting side by side, and I wondered if I had imagined the whole thing. He was gone when I came back to the house, and Grandma was sitting, her hands folded in her lap, gazing out across the lake.

A little later she called from the porch, "Eve. Would you mind . . . I hate asking you . . . but . . . I almost forgot. Dave said in his last letter for me to have you go to the courthouse and pay the second half of the taxes. It's open until four. Could you go today?"

"Sure," Mom answered. "I'll go this afternoon. I should pick up some groceries anyway."

Grandma summoned me to the porch the moment Mom left the driveway. I wasn't surprised, but I was curious.

"Another ride?" I teased.

"No. A walk. Up the stairs."

"You've got to be kidding. Just tell me what you want, and I'll get it."

"It's not that simple. It's something I have to do myself, but I can't do it alone. I need your help. It's in my bedroom."

"How are we going to manage?"

She was standing in the porch doorway. "Help me to the bottom of the stairs and I'll show you."

I steadied her and we made our way down the hall. The stairs looked as enormous as they had when I was a child.

"Now if I sit on the bottom step and you sit on the step behind me, and when I say pull, you lift me up and back up a step—it may take a while, but we'll get there."

"I know," I said. "You always finish what you start."

I pulled. We bumped and panted and heaved our way up the long, long flight of stairs to the landing, where we rested.

"Are you sure it's worth it, Wyn? We'll still have to go back down."

"I'm sure. Pull me around, and I'll be ready for the last few steps."

"Okay. If you say so."

"I do, indeed, say so."

I gave another pull.

When we got to the top, I helped her to her feet and we walked slowly down the hall to her bedroom.

"In the chest in the corner. There's a green steel box.

The key is taped under the chest. There by that back leg."

I found the box and the key and brought them to her. She opened it and took out a bunch of letters. "Put it back where you found it. This is what I came for."

Going down was easier. Grandma had me get a pillow, and I sat on the step behind her, my arms around her as we bumped our way slowly down the stairs.

"Now what?" I asked as we sat at the bottom of the steps in the glow of the stained glass window.

"Get some matches. We're going to have a fire in the fireplace."

I pulled a chair over to the hearth. She sat down and carefully untied the bundle of letters. I saw her name on the top one—written with a hyphen: Wyn Rhys-Roberts. There was no return address.

"You know," she said, striking a match and carefully lighting the edge of the first envelope, "everyone has a corner of life that is private. Most of us hold on to the remnants as long as we can. But there comes a time for . . . for . . ."

"Thinning out?"

"Plucking out," she said.

We didn't talk again, while one by one she burned the letters and watched them curl into black ash.

I wanted to ask who the letters were from, but there was something in my grandmother's face that stopped me.

After I helped her back to the porch, she asked if I would clean out the fireplace.

Mom walked in a half hour later.

"What's that smell? Is something burning?" she asked.

"No," Grandma said. "The burning is over." Her voice left no room for questions.

Uncle Dave came the next week. He was not the most exciting person in the world. He was nice enough and always asked the right kind of questions, but he never waited for the answers.

"David is like his father," Grandma said. I wasn't sure if it were a compliment or not.

While he was with us, he and Mom and Grandma spent a lot of time together with bankbooks, insurance policies and the shopping bag Grandma had me bring up from the basement marked in crayon: "Important Papers."

My uncle finally left, taking with him the silver service, the Haviland china, and the brass candlesticks from Wales.

"They've always gone to the oldest son," Grandma explained.

It was nice to have the house to ourselves again. We fell back into the same routine. Mom worked, I played golf, and Vi dropped in.

It still amazed me that Grandma and Vi could sit out on the back porch for two or three hours every day and find something to laugh and talk about after forty years of knowing each other. I never really listened to their conversation because I felt I would be intruding. Not that they deliberately made me feel that way, but whatever they talked about consumed their entire attention. I always felt as if I were alone when they were together.

And that's how I had started to feel with Lew—as if I were alone when we were together. It was as if he were treating me like a little sister and I didn't know how to stop it. Or maybe with the golf tournament coming up, he was behaving as if he were my teacher. I could think of a lot of things I would rather have him teach me than how to make a chip shot roll when it hits the green or how to play an uphill putt.

But one day Lew finally asked me to do something besides play golf.

"A picnic? Tonight?" I hoped I didn't sound as excited as I felt. I would have gone on a bird walk with Gladys and him if he'd suggested that.

We rowed across the lake, in the late afternoon, and Lew beached the boat at Wyn Rhys Park.

"Have you ever been here?"

"Just once," I replied. "With Mom."

There were probably a dozen other places around the lake where we might have gone, and he'd chosen Grandma's park. I wondered if he thought we needed a chaperone.

"They keep this a primitive area. Trails wind back for miles. When your grandmother gave this land to the public, she insisted that it be left in its virgin state."

"That's nice," I said, wishing he'd chosen a different adjective and a different park!

"It's really a wildlife refuge. Hardly anyone comes here much. Only nature lovers."

I liked those words better.

We unloaded the boat and followed the shoreline to a small grassy hill that rose out of the trees. Lew spread a blanket and we sat down.

"This is the best spot on the lake to watch the sun set."

The sun set.

Lew built a fire.

"Were you a Boy Scout?" I asked. I might as well have been with Kim.

"Boy Scouts don't bring wine in their knapsacks—and Virene's fried chicken. Are you hungry?"

"Not yet. I like just sitting here." I didn't add, "With you." Kim would have been proud of me. I was thinking before I was talking.

He stretched out beside me and leaned on one elbow. "This hasn't been a very good summer for you, has it? For any of you? You must miss your friends." He sounded like Uncle David.

"I have my golf. At least my game's improving. And there's no one at home who's that important, anyway. What about you? You must find Preston pretty dull."

"It's been a good summer, really. Met a lot of old friends I knew as a kid. Met new ones too."

I waited for him to go on, but he didn't. I wanted him to say, "I met *you*." I thought about the time we'd spent together—the walk after dinner that first night, the mornings at the golf course, the night at the game reserve. Something was different now. There was a kind of tension between us that hadn't been there before.

"What are you thinking about?" I asked, wanting to trace the outline of his face with my fingers.

"That summer will be over soon. That I'll be leaving. That we probably won't see each other again."

"Do you mind?"

"I mind. How often does a Rhys come along?" He sat up, rummaged through his back pack, and pulled out the wine bottle. "Let's open this before it gets warm."

He poured the wine into Styrofoam cups and, when he handed me mine, his fingers brushed against my hand. I wondered if he'd done it deliberately, but it didn't really matter. The feeling was lovely. He hadn't touched me since that night at the Colby House.

Suddenly, I knew what was wrong.

"My being sixteen bothers you, doesn't it?"

"Don't be silly. Of course not."

I didn't say any more. I just looked at him.

He glanced down at his wine, swished it around in the cup and grinned. "Yeah," he muttered. "Sixteen is a beautiful age, but . . ."

"But dangerous?"

"Dangerous if you're twenty-six."

"You don't have to be afraid. I'm not."

I felt as if I were standing on the high diving tower. Up there, you can see all over the beach and around the lake. Everything is clear and defined and exciting. There's fear, too, of actually diving, but once you're in the air, the fear disappears.

"I've been waiting for you," I said.

His hand covered mine, his fingers encircling my wrist. "Why?"

"Why? Because you're you. The way you look. The things you say. The way you smell. And taste. And your teeth are beautiful."

"My teeth!" He lay down and pulled me toward him.

"I think teeth are important." My voice was husky.

The fire crackled, sending out tiny sparks that arched through the gathering dark. He held my face away from his so we were looking into each other's eyes.

"Oh, Rhys. My teeth?"

"Teeth," I said as I leaned closer to him, "have always been very important to me."

A few minutes later I had forgotten all about teeth.

We finished the wine. We lay together on the blanket and stared up at the stars and talked until it was very late.

Virene's fried chicken went uneaten.

We rowed back across the lake and left the tree locusts and frogs to enjoy the virgin state of Wyn Rhys Park.

The house was dark when I walked in. In a way I was sorry. I would have liked to have talked to Mom, to have shared what I was feeling. She was a woman. She would have understood.

It was Grandma who called to me from the darkened porch.

She was sitting in her chair looking out across the lake.

"I saw Lew bring you back."

I waited for the questions to begin.

"Just for tonight, Rhys, and just for a moment, I wished I could have changed places with you. The night. The lake. And someone very special."

"What makes you think he's special?"

"Because," she said quietly, "you're my granddaughter."

13

Decisions

"How did it all happen?"

Grandma's conversations often started in the middle.

"What do you mean, Mother?"

Mom and I were sitting with her. The day had been dark and overcast and now heavy clouds hung low over the lake, hiding the fringe of trees that marked the far shore so that the lake looked as if it extended into the horizon.

"Getting old. When do you know you're getting old? It seems like it was just last week I was Rhys's age and only yesterday I was your age, Eve. And here I am old!"

"I understand, Mother. The inside and the outside don't match anymore."

"I know," Grandma agreed. "That's the way I feel now. The trouble is we never believe it's going to happen to us. The growing old, I mean. And when it does, it's such a shock."

128

"Yes," Mom said. "I'm forty-two, but it never seems quite real. It's as if a part of me stays Rhys's age, no matter how many years pass."

It was hard to believe. I felt exactly the age I was—sixteen, which, if you've ever been sixteen, you know is sometimes great and sometimes awful. Even Lew hadn't changed that. I didn't much like the prospect of staying sixteen for the rest of my life.

"Eve, were you ever sixteen? I always thought you were going on thirty-five when you were five. You were a loner. You still are." Grandma tilted her head and looked across at Mom. "Have you ever thought of getting married again? Or living with a man? I know it isn't a necessity, but it can be a luxury."

The same question had occurred to me several times, but only Grandma would put it into words.

I looked at Mom and grinned. "What an interesting question."

"You two would be surprised at the things I've thought of over the years." She laughed.

"I doubt it, Eve." Grandma sighed. "I've spent eighty years being a woman and I've thought of just about everything."

"Thinking and doing are two different things. You didn't remarry."

"No. I might have. But it would have been for the wrong reasons."

"What are the right reasons?" I asked.

"One is to make yourself *twice* what you could have been alone," Grandma said firmly. "Unfortunately, sometimes it makes you *half* of what you might have been."

"Then you understand, Mother," Mom said slowly as if choosing each word carefully, "why I never remarried. I married the first time for the wrong reason. To prove I was an adult. But I wasn't. And when I grew up . . . well, things didn't work any more."

I wondered why Mom and I had never talked about this.

"I understand how you feel, Mom," I said, "but if you met someone now, someone you really liked . . . and just sort of wanted to live with . . . to see . . . to try it out . . . well, I wouldn't mind. At least I don't think I would."

"I would, Rhys, if it were *you*."

Mom was not laughing now.

"Oh, Mom." I groaned. "You're just thinking about sex."

"Notice, Eve." Grandma chuckled. "Rhys can even say the word. There's hope for the world after all. When I married your father, I didn't know anything. Neither did he. At least, Eve, I tried to tell you the facts, but I was never sure you understood the poetry."

Grandma had used the right word. It *was* poetry. That's what I had felt with Lew.

"I guess you're right, Mother," Mom said softly. "Maybe I never understood the poetry. I was too busy working, and then there was graduate school. There hasn't been time."

"Then you must learn, Eve, that the poetry doesn't fade with age. If anything, it becomes lovelier. More intense."

"It does?" I asked. "I thought after menopause . . ."

"I take back what I said about hope for the world"—Grandma shook her head—"if that's what you believe."

I remembered that brief glimpse of Grandma and Reverend Baddeley standing together on the porch.

130

"Yes, I suppose the poetry is there," Mom admitted, "but these last few years I've had to make choices. To decide on my priorities."

"Meaning me?" I asked.

Mom leaned toward me. "In part. But you have to understand, Rhys, it has been *my* choice. It's been what I've wanted. I have not wanted to be involved . . . sexually involved with anyone. Perhaps that will change, but not just now."

If Mom thought she was still sixteen, she was mistaken.

"Then you know the most important thing, Eve." Grandma settled back in her chair. "That there are choices. That there are many ways of living . . . and of loving . . . and of being happy." She was talking to Mom, but she was looking at me.

Mom glanced at her watch. "It's late. I'll fix us something for dinner."

"Don't bother, Eve," Grandma said, getting up slowly from her chair and walking to the window. She stood with her back to us, her forehead pressed against the screen. "I'm not hungry tonight. Maybe later. I want to talk."

I thought the three of us had talked about everything there was to talk about, except the one thing that none of us wanted to put into words.

"What is it, Mother?" Mom asked. "Is anything wrong?"

Grandma managed a half chuckle. "Do you really want me to answer that, Eve?"

Mother was learning to absorb Grandma's remarks without wincing.

"I want to talk to both of you," Grandma began, still

131

looking out across the lake, "about what dying feels like."

I wanted to say, "Oh no," but the strength in her voice stopped me.

"It's a strange learning," she said, calmly. "Last year, when the doctor first told me, I simply didn't believe it. 'Not me!' I protested. 'It couldn't be!' Maybe because in my mind I was the same person I'd always been."

Mom started to get up from her chair. Grandma turned from the window to face us. "Then I fell on the stairs. After that I had time to think. I was angry. Angry at the world. 'Why me?' And I was still angry when you came this summer. I was not going to let it happen."

All the fierceness of Twtti Wyn Hec showed in her eyes.

"After I came home again, I bargained with whatever runs the world. 'Just give me this summer. One summer will be enough.' But you see. One summer is not enough. I want the fall and the winter too and who can resist spring? Now I know that, no matter what I want, it is not going to happen. That learning took a long time.

"A time comes when you consider all the options, including suicide. For some it may be right, but not for me. I finish what I begin. I made one mistake, though."

"Just one, Mother?" Mom said with a slight smile.

"Eve!" Grandma smiled back. "If you're not careful, you're going to develop as nasty a sense of humor as mine!"

I heard more tenderness behind their words than I had ever heard before.

"The mistake was expecting that it would be easier to die here. Eve, you don't know what it is going to be like. The doctor was right. I should go back to the nursing home. I'm failing every day. I feel it. I'm tired most of the time. It is such an effort to move, and I know it will get worse. I don't want you and Rhys to have to care for a mindless body in a bed for the rest of the time. Take me back to the hospital."

At last I felt the grief of my grandma's dying, and I could see it mirrored in my mother's eyes.

"No," Mom said so gently that I could hardly hear. "We all belong here—together."

The next day, Vi and Shrimp McKinley moved a hospital bed onto the porch.

133

14

A Hot August

A battered pick-up truck pulled into the drive one hot August Friday. Vi climbed out from behind the wheel and helped Lew and a short man whom Vi called "Buell-Hon" to unload a heavy crate.

"Is Wynnie up yet? Brought her a surprise."

"She's sitting in her chair," I answered from the front door.

"Good. Got an air-conditioner. We're coming through."

And they did, right through to the sleeping porch, Vi and Lew, red-faced and sweating, balancing the heavy crate between them, and Buell-Hon trailing behind with a small tool kit.

"Hernia," Vi whispered out of the side of her mouth as the two set the air-conditioner down in front of Grandma.

"What did you do that for, Vi?" Grandma protested.

"Because I felt like it. Reason enough. This hot spell's

supposed to last for two more weeks. I'm not going to have you melting down like soft butter. Besides, I get a discount on appliances. Third husband, remember?"

Lew and Buell-Hon installed the air conditioner, Vi gave instructions, while Grandma, Mom and I watched.

"No. The brace goes this way. And Buell-Hon, don't lift that. Let me do it. Not that way, Lew. The other way." She turned to Grandma, "Corncrib carpenters. Both of them."

"Vi, you didn't have to go to all this bother," Grandma said.

"You've bothered with me for forty years," Vi replied, touching Grandma's shoulder. "It's my turn now."

Grandma reached up and caught Vi's hand and held it for a moment. "I wish we had another forty years."

Vi looked down at her and turned quickly. "Now, boys, be sure that window's tight around. Otherwise it's a waste." She spoke directly to me. "Now, I know Wyn can't abide closed windows, but heat like this . . . well . . . during the day, if you'll pull the blinds and leave this thing on"—she gestured at the air conditioner—"well, you can probably open up the place at night."

Her eyes held tears, but she didn't cry, and I pretended not to see.

Mom leaned over and touched my arm. "Rhys, could you—would you make some tea or lemonade for Lew and Buell . . . Buell"—I knew she stopped herself before she said Buell-Hon—"and the rest of us."

"Lemonade?" Grandma said. "Why I haven't had that in years. Not the real kind. At the home they gave out something that came from a can. If that was lemonade, I'm Twtti Glyn Hec."

Without stopping to think that she might have for-

135

gotten, I said, "It's Twtti *Wyn* Hec—don't you remember?"

"Remember! Of course I remember. *I* changed the name to fit *me*. It's really Twtti *Glyn* Hec."

"What are you two picking at each other about?" Vi sat beside Grandma, "You boys clean up that mess you made."

"I'm just owning up to an ancient lie." Grandma pointed toward Lew. "Hand me your broom, and I'll show you. You see, Vi, I could never bear to spank the children when they were naughty, so I scared them to death instead. Made them think I was a witch." Grasping the broom in one hand, she sang in a thin crackly voice:

> The sprites of Glyn Mawddy
> Will wring my old neck
> If anyone discovers
> I'm Twtti Glyn Hec.

"Now that's authentic. But I changed it to Wyn to make believers of them. It worked. Never did have to spank them. And it worked on Rhys too when she was little." She laughed the old witch laugh and I felt the same goosebumps again.

"I'll get the lemonade right away," I said, and Grandma laughed in her own voice.

After the lemonade, with the air conditioner humming softly, Grandma napped. Vi and Buell-Hon left and Lew stayed to prune the bushes outside the porch windows.

After he finished, he joined Mom and me at the kitchen table. The kitchen had become the center of our lives. We never left Grandma completely alone. Mom even brought her work down, and we sort of took turns being near.

"I was thinking the other day," Mom said, "how strange, that in a house this big, we always lived in the kitchen and on the porch. And it hasn't changed."

"Probably because you can see the lake," I suggested.

"It provides the basic needs: food and beauty. What else is there, really?" Lew asked.

"That sounds like something Mother would say," Mom commented.

"She did, last week."

Lew's arm was draped across the back of my chair and while we talked his fingers made lazy circles on my shoulder. Whatever sense of competition I'd had with Mom had disappeared.

"It's good that you could be here this summer," Mom said. "You've made it easier for Virene."

"I'm glad you think so, but I'm not sure anything will help very much. The most important thing is that you and Rhys were here." He smiled at Mom. "But then you two would be important anywhere."

I reached behind me and squeezed his wrist. "Don't believe him, Mom. He's part Irish, remember? And full of blarney. You should hear him with the women at the pro shop." I turned toward him and lowered my voice, imitating him. "Now, Midge, you have a lovely swing when you walk. If you could just try the same thing when you're teeing off."

Mom laughed and Lew rapped my jaw lightly. "Eve, how could a lovely person like you have a daughter like Rhys?"

"Don't blame me. Blame her grandmother. You should

know that by now." Mom's smile faded. "How long will you be staying? When do you have to leave?"

I was glad Mom put it into words even though I didn't want to hear the answer. It was a summer of endings. Or was it a summer of beginnings? And was there really any difference? I thought of Grandma's painting. Maybe there couldn't be one without the other. One thing I knew. There would have to be something of Lew in anyone I could ever love.

Lew's hand touched the back of my neck. "That's something I haven't wanted to think about. But in a couple of weeks, I guess. I hadn't planned to stay even this long."

"Rhys!" Grandma called from the porch.

I jumped up and hurried to the door, Lew and Mom behind me.

"Shut this contraption off! I can't hear a word you're saying."

Grandma's world was soon limited to the hospital bed and her air-conditioned porch. Mom and I became experts at bed-making, food-serving, and patient-watching. Grandma still insisted on sitting in her chair for a few hours each day, while she read.

She stopped listening to the radio; she refused to watch television, but oh, how she read. Not new books from the library, nor magazines, but the old books she asked me to bring down from upstairs, some in English, some in Welsh.

The days were quiet. Mom worked at the kitchen table, Grandma read on the porch, I still played golf every morning. Vi came over for a little while every afternoon and sometimes Lew was there in the evening.

Uncle David called every night. It was as if we were waiting for a guest to arrive.

We were out on her porch, the big, glassed-in room that looked down over the lawn to the lake. She was propped up in the hospital bed, which she still hated, her body so small it looked as if the bed were empty. Her hands, wrinkled and freckled, lay still upon the sheet, thumbs tucked into palms like a baby's. I sat beside her in one of her old white wicker chairs. Mom was upstairs resting.

"Rhys. Look. The moon is melting."

The full moon, low and red over the lake, did look as if it were melting and running down across the water.

"You said that once. When you were only four."

"I did?"

"Yes, you did. It was Thanksgiving. You and Eve and all of Dave's family were here. The house was full, and I needed a moment by myself. Taking the garbage out was always a good excuse."

I could remember a Christmas, but I could not remember a Thanksgiving.

"You followed me out of the house in your nightgown and robe and overshoes. I said, 'What on earth are you doing out here?' And you put your hand in mine and said, 'I *need* you, Grandma.' So we stood and looked up at the moon through the pines and the mist and then you said, 'Grandma, the moon is melting.' From that time on you were special to me."

"I don't remember that. Now, I don't think I'll ever forget."

I knew it was getting late, but Grandma didn't seem sleepy, so I stayed.

"Is there anything of mine you would like, Rhys?"

I had felt bad enough at the beginning of the summer about dividing and selling Grandma's things. It was worse now. It sounded so final.

"There are some good antiques in there. Those Welsh brass lanterns. Belonged to my grandfather. He was a miner. They're valuable now. I've some jewelry in my safe deposit box in the bank. We could get it out and look it over. That grandfather clock in the hall, but I don't know where on earth you'd put it in your house."

"The only thing I'd like," I said, "is the painting in the front room. The one you did of the lake. When did you do it?"

"Once when I had to make a decision."

Grandma was quiet for a long time.

"Rhys. Come here for just a minute. I'd like to hold you. I haven't done that for a long time."

I sat on the edge of the bed and she put her arms around me, but she wasn't holding me. I was holding her.

15

The Little Amenities

The news of Grandma's illness and our staying on spread throughout Preston, and with the knowledge came the flowers and cards and visitors.

She hated hothouse plants. "It's like keeping animals in a zoo. Things should be where they naturally belong. Plants shouldn't be stuck in a clay pot, dribbled up with aluminum foil, and held with plastic sticks."

So when the front doorbell rang and the florist arrived, Grandma would look at the card, comment "that was nice" and point toward the herb garden. "Set it out there on the edge. Don't know why they didn't use their wits and send seeds instead. Gardening is the process of growth, not the product."

The cut flowers infuriated her. "They'll only last a day or two. What makes people think I want to sit and watch them die?" The flowers were exiled to the front parlor with a wave of Grandma's hand.

Cards fared no better. "Insipid, aren't they? 'Get well

soon.' 'Sorry to hear you're ill.' What they should say is, 'I'm glad it isn't me'."

One day after I'd given her almost a dozen cards that came in the morning mail, I came back to the porch to see if she wanted some tea. She was lying propped up in the bed, slowly dropping the unopened envelopes, one by one, into the wastebasket beside the bed.

She hesitated, then handed one to me. "This might be worth reading. Open it."

I carefully slit the envelope. Grandma did not like her mail ripped open. The stationery was thick and creamy, with a building embossed at the top. I said, "It's from the bank, I think."

Grandma looked closer. "It's from Dorothy. APW's been dead for thirty-five years. She still uses his left-over bank stationery."

The handwriting was like engraving.

Dear Wyn,
Wanda and Albert and I have rented a two-bed-room, ground floor apartment down on Willow Street and we're all going to live there together.
Come and see us when we get moved in.

Love,
Dorothy

Grandma closed her eyes and smiled. "Dorothy was always a slow learner, but at least she learned before it was too late."

"Learned what?"

"How to bend . . . how to love."

Visitors were different from cards. They couldn't be disposed of quite so easily, but Grandma did work out a system. When a caller came, Mom or I would say, "Let

142

me see if she's sleeping," and we'd hurry out to the porch and tell Grandma who it was. Then she'd decide whether they should be allowed to stay five, ten, or, rarely, fifteen minutes.

When I asked how she ranked them she said, "Like eggs. Soft, poached, or deviled. Deviled takes longer."

Only Virene and Lew came unannounced and stayed until Grandma told them she was tired.

Occasionally, they came in the evening. Grandma often had trouble getting to sleep, so we'd all sit on the porch with her in the coolness of the night. Grandma insisted that all the windows be opened so she could hear the lake lapping against the shore.

"Let's have a poker game," Vi suggested. "Do you know how to play, Eve?"

"Yes," Mom said. "Mother taught me. Do you feel up to playing, Mother?"

"No, I'd rather kibbitz. Pull the table over here where I can see." It was late, but Grandma was still sitting in her chair.

"Your grandmother is one sharp poker player, Rhys." Virene lifted the table and carried it across the room before Lew could get to his feet to help. "Remember that lot, Wynnie?" She turned to us. "She won a vacant lot on Bullhead Drive from Harley Strum one night at the Moose Lodge. Sold it back to him ten years later at a profit."

"You never told me about that, Mother," Mom said.

Grandma laughed. "Mothers don't always tell their daughters everything."

"Where are the cards and chips?" Lew asked.

"In the hall closet," Grandma answered. "But let's really sweeten the pot tonight. Vi, you always did have your eye on my eighty acres south of town. And I wouldn't mind having that duplex you built."

"For real?" I exclaimed, thankful that I didn't own anything.

"No, for fun. Vi and I have been doing it for years. More exciting than nickels and dimes. Now let's see. Lew has his car . . ."

"He can have the pro shop too," Vi interrupted. "It'd net about four thousand dollars for the summer. How about you, Eve?"

Mom rubbed her forehead. "Well, there's the house, and the car is new. I suppose I could let Rhys use the certificates of deposit."

"No." Grandma's voice was excited. "Rhys and I will be in this together. I'll stake her to all my holdings."

"But, Wyn," I objected, "I've never played before."

"Then it's high time you learned. And it won't cost you a dime."

By the time the evening was over, Lew had lost everything he owned, but he had won Mom's house and Vi's truck stop. Mom managed to hang onto her car and added the duplex, the beauty parlor and two of Vi's lakeshore cottages. I had lost everything—Grandma's farms, all her stocks and bonds, even her life insurance policy. Everything except the house.

"One last hand," Vi said. "Rhys still has the house. I always did like this place, Wyn."

"Go ahead, Rhys, bet it all," Grandma urged. "Never quit, even when you're losing. Bet the furnishings too."

"But, Wyn, I can't."

"Come on, girl," Vi ordered. "You're holding up the game."

"It's just for fun, Rhys." Mom was fingering the card face down before her. "It's only a game."

"Go ahead," Grandma insisted. "Our luck is bound to change."

"Can I bet just the garage?"

"It's not enough to cover," Mom warned.

"You'll have to bet all or nothing," Grandma whispered, her lips brushing my ear. "It's up to you. Do you want to chance it?"

Lew didn't say anything. He just smiled across at me, but I was sure he understood what I was feeling. The trouble was, it wasn't a game anymore. All I could think of was Grandma's voice that afternoon at Sunset Haven when she had said, "I'm going home."

"No!" I pushed the cards away. "I fold. I won't lose Grandma's house."

"Well," Grandma said, and I thought she sounded surprised. Then she went on. "I think it's probably time for me to be in bed anyway."

The game ended, Lew and Vi left, Mom went upstairs to bed and I was about to follow, when Grandma called.

"Rhys, would you bring me some stationery and an envelope? They're in the desk in the parlor."

"Do you want me to stay till you finish?" I asked.

"No, I'll turn off the light. But I'd like you to take a letter to the post office in the morning. Send it registered mail."

I sent the letter the next day. It was addressed to my Uncle Dave.

16

The Last Lesson

L ew and I were together twice a day, every day now, as the Ladies' Open Golf Tournament drew nearer. I still played eighteen holes in the morning early, and then, if we timed it right, we were able to squeeze in nine holes over the 6 P.M. dinner hour when the course wasn't crowded.

It was the evening before the three-day event. I wouldn't be playing my qualifying round until the second day, so this was our last round, nine holes, before the competition. Rain had been threatening all afternoon and by the time Lew and I got to the fifth hole, it had started to drizzle.

"A good golfer plays in any weather. Let's keep going. And keep your drives quail-high."

After my summer in Preston I knew what he meant. A quail never flies more than five to ten feet off the ground, and Lew had taught me how to place the shoe of my club at the correct angle.

"It's how far your drives go—not how high," he continually warned me. Before I met Lew, most of my drives arched like rainbows down the fairway.

My shot off the fifth hole exploded quail-high and landed on the green.

"Why do you always have to be right?" I grumbled.

"Because I'm twenty-six," he answered, dropping his drive just feet from mine, but closer to the pin.

"All that means is that you're going to be old before I am," I teased.

"I'm working on that. A way for you to catch up, or me to slow down. I'll fill you in when I get the formula. If you'll keep—let me know where you are."

A month ago I would have been embarrassed talking about our ages, but now it wasn't important, because I had learned something about age, and not just from Lew. Grandma had said, "Age isn't measured in years. Look at the trees. They're measured in growth rings." Maybe in growth rings, I was already catching up with Lew.

We both parred the hole, but just as we reached the sixth, the drizzle burst into a downpour. We huddled under the shelter, closed off by a silver curtain. We were more alone than we had ever been.

I waited for him to put his arm around me, but he didn't. Instead he sat hunched beside me, staring into the rain. It was as if the curtain had dropped between us.

"Rhys. There's something more I want to tell you."

"I know. It was my last putt, wasn't it?"

"No. Not your putt. It went in, didn't it? No, what I was thinking was that maybe, after this tournament is over, we could have dinner together. Sunday."

147

"Sure. Colby House?"

"No, I thought we'd drive into Cummings. You see, Rhys, I have to leave on Monday."

I had known all summer that this had to happen, but I didn't know there could be such a heavy emptiness in me, as if something had sucked all the air from my lungs, leaving only a vacuum.

"You know"—his hand covered mine—"I hoped you'd leave first."

I could get out only one word: "Why?"

"It's harder to be left than to leave."

We sat holding each other.

"Leaving isn't easy either," he went on. "I'm going to spend the rest of my life searching for a Rhys."

"There's only one of me," I said with certainty.

"I know." Lew's voice was choked. "That's what's wrong."

The rain stopped, and for the first time that summer we did not finish the round.

The next day I spent swimming off the dock, lying in the sun, and thinking about life without Lew. I finally decided there was no use in thinking. There was nothing I could do. There was nothing he could do, and I didn't want Mom and Grandma to know how I felt. But I would see Lew at the tournament and we would have one more evening together. It really couldn't end until it was over.

That night when only the three of us were home, Grandma leaned back in her chair and said, "Do you know what I'd like? More than anything else in the world?"

"What is it, Mother?" Mom looked up from her book.

"It's not much, really. My wants have finally matched

my needs. I want to go down to my garden again, by the lake. I don't need to do anything. I just want to sit. Outside."

Mom closed her book. I thought I knew what she was going to say, but she surprised me. "Why not? It's a lovely evening, and the breeze will be cool. Do you mind if we come along?"

Grandma attempted a laugh. "How else would I get there? If you mean, can you stay, of course you can."

"Rhys, you carry a lawn chair down first. And then come back and help us."

The walk to the herb garden took a long time. We moved slowly, Grandma between us, our arms around her. I knew she had lost weight, but I didn't realize how much. There's a big difference between seeing it and feeling it. Holding her was like holding a bird, light and brittle.

We sat in the dusk, Grandma in the lawn chair, Mom and I in the grass at her feet, and watched the evening settle on the lake. We were a triangle, and Grandma was the apex.

"That's Venus, the evening star," Grandma said. "I've always thought the first star is so much more exciting than the sunrise."

"Do you remember, Mother, when I was a child you told me that it was made especially for me?"

"Of course I remember, Eve. Maybe things like evening stars and views of the lake and the night sky are the best memories of all. You can't be sure where one ends and another begins."

I lay back in the grass and watched the sky.

"My mother used to tell me that back in Wales there was a well that when you threw a garment in, you could

tell by the way it sank whether a sick person would re-
cover. It was probably as accurate as a doctor. There is
something about water—about a lake—that is mystic."

"I know," I agreed, "but I don't understand why."

"If I were treating it academically," Mom said, "I'd
probably call it the collective unconscious, but really, I
think it's the motion—the wind on the water—the constant change, like life."

"Yes, there's that," Grandma agreed, "but something
more. There's a knowing that comes when you live by
water."

"Knowing what?" I asked.

"I can't tell you . . . You will learn." Grandma's
voice was almost a whisper.

We sat without talking for a while, then Grandma said,
"I have a feeling that I'll never really leave this house.
Part of me will always be here."

"For a Welsh witch, that shouldn't be too difficult."
Mom was teasing gently.

"It's a pity I couldn't pass the power on to you, Eve.
Rhys has it, you know."

"Yes," Mom said. "And I'm glad."

I sat up on my knees, imitating Grandma's cackly
voice.

> The sprites of Glen Mawddy
> Will wring my old neck
> If anyone discovers
> I'm Twtti *Rhys* Hec.

Both of them laughed. In their laughter I heard the
backward echo of my own, Mom's strong and controlled,
Grandma's weak and frail, and for the first time I under-

stood that part of me would die with Grandma, but part of her would live in me.

"Eve, I haven't told David yet, nor you, but I have told Rhys. I don't intend to be buried. I hope you don't mind."

Mom turned toward me with a questioning look.

"Grandma donated her body to the medical school," I said.

"I've enjoyed this body for eighty years. Maybe it'll help somebody else enjoy theirs a little longer. The ashes will be sent to Vi. Vi's got common sense about things like that. She's promised to sprinkle them over my herb garden. It won't hurt the plants."

"It's a lovely idea, Mother," Mom said. Her voice was honest. "Do you want me to tell Dave?"

"Either you or Rhys. It won't matter."

"What does Reverend Baddeley think? Or did you tell him?"

Grandma folded her arms and leaned back in the chair. "He approved. He should. He suggested it. Said he could keep track of me that way."

We all three laughed again, our voices blending into one.

"Would you like a bath, Mother?" Mom asked as we got back to the porch. "It was warm out there."

"It's so much trouble. I don't believe so tonight. Maybe just a cool wash cloth, if you don't mind bringing one." She didn't want to sit in her chair; instead, she lay back on the bed.

When I looked at her, I thought of the part in *Alice in Wonderland*, where Alice eats the thing that makes her shrink. It was as if, small as she was when we'd walked

151

down to the lake, she had grown even smaller on the way back.

"But you can have a bath, Wyn." I'm not sure where the words came from because I hadn't thought about them before. "Mom and I can help. We can give you a bath right in bed." I had never helped bathe anyone in my life, except Kim's poodle, but I thought it couldn't be too hard. Besides, she *was* my grandmother.

"Of course, Mother. It won't take long. Besides, think how many times you must have washed me. And Rhys too. Do you remember? When I brought her home as a baby, you always wanted to bathe her. That was when I thought you really might steal her away."

"How do you know it won't work the other way around? I might steal her *this* time."

Grandma lay still with her eyes closed as we washed her. I had never wanted to be a nurse. I knew that I'd never want to do the things that were part of the job, like giving baths to all sorts of people I didn't even know. But somehow this was different and I didn't mind at all.

Grandma did not go back down to her lake again.

17

Competition

Tee-off time for my qualifying round was set at
8 A.M. I biked out early, thinking I'd have a little
time alone with Lew. It wasn't that I needed any last-
minute instructions. I just wanted to be with him one
extra time.

He was already sitting behind the registration desk,
looking just as gorgeous as he had the first day I met him.
Obviously I wasn't the only one who thought so because
he was surrounded by women golfers, all sizes, all ages,
all shapes. I stood back and watched. One of the nicest
things about Lew was that he never seemed to realize how
attractive he was.

When my turn came, he didn't bother to look up until
I said, "Are sixteen-year-olds allowed to enter this
tournament? My name is Rhys."

He grinned up at me. "Only if they know how to
play. Do you have your own clubs?"

"Yes, sir. And I've even been taking lessons . . . from an *old* pro."

"Don't be impudent to your elders." He handed me my card. "Did you know that part of the prize is that I play the winner Sunday morning and take her out to dinner Sunday night?"

"I'll bet she didn't know that until she entered the tournament."

"She does now. Do you think you can remember?"

A line had formed behind me, and I moved on toward the clubhouse. Remember? Remember? Remember? All my life I had never thought anything was important enough to remember. Now there was something in my life that I could never forget. Maybe that's what growing up was. Beginning to remember.

I found a table on the far corner of the patio and watched other golfers arrive. Their clubs and bags and carts looked so professional that, if I hadn't loved the game, I would have scratched and gone home.

A short, stocky woman whose hair spun out in red-gold wisps, walked up.

"Rhys?"

I nodded.

"That beautiful young man over there said we're on the same card. I'm Marian. Mind if I sit down for a minute? The rest of our foursome isn't here yet. They're never on time anyway."

She eased herself into a metal chair—her body settling into a series of circles.

"You've played with them before?" I asked.

"Sure. Known them for years. I'm probably the oldest one here. You're probably the youngest. The other two, Sally and Eula, are lost somewhere in between."

Eula and Sally arrived at the last minute. Once we were on the course I couldn't see that Marian was having any trouble. She didn't hit the ball very far, but every shot was a straight line to the hole.

Eula, tall and frizzy-haired, about mother's age, looked like a professional athlete. She hit powerful, soaring drives that disappeared down the fairway. We seldom saw her until we were all on the green.

Sally, a suburban social type, wore a shoulder-length pageboy and dark circles under her eyes.

On every hole, Sally spent most of her time in the rough.

"You're a good golfer, Rhys," Marian said as she steered our cart under a shade tree to wait while Sally looked for her lost ball. "How come we haven't met before?"

"I don't live in Preston. Mom and I are just here for the summer."

"Visiting?"

"Staying with my grandmother."

"Oh. You must be—why of course. I should have recognized the name. I bet you're Wyn Rhys's granddaughter."

"How'd you know?" I asked.

"Everybody knows your grandmother. And the Rhys name of course. She was a top-notch golfer in her day. In fact, she was one of the charter members of the club."

"Grandma? You must be wrong. She's never said anything about it and neither has Mom."

"She won this tournament one year. The first year it was ever played. Something must have happened. She never played again."

"I bet I know why," I said as I waved back at Sally, who had just located her ball. "She wanted to find out if she could do it, and when she found she could, she stopped."

"That's crazy."

"My grandmother is an . . . unusual person." I remembered Grandma's comments about hitting a ball around a pasture. She hadn't been teasing me. She was laughing at herself.

"Maybe I'm crazier than your grandmother. I play golf just to see if I can get from one hole to the other. I mean if I blow one hole, I always can start over on the next." She selected an iron and dropped an approach ten feet from the hole. I followed. My ball skittered past the flag leaving me a healthy fifteen-footer to par.

Marian and I qualified for the afternoon championship flight.

I biked home for lunch, taking my time on the road that wound around the lake, thinking about my putting. I had missed a couple "gimme's" that Lew would have teased me about.

The doctor's car was parked in front of Grandma's house. He had been stopping in once a week, but this was the wrong day.

I ran up the front steps. Mom had seen me coming and was waiting for me.

"What's wrong?"

"She's having trouble breathing. She's in pain."

"What does he say?"

"I don't know. We haven't had a chance to talk." I followed Mom back to the kitchen.

"Do you think . . . this is . . . ?" I didn't know how to finish.

156

"It's so strange," Mom went on as if she hadn't heard me. "You accept—in your mind—and then when it begins to happen, you find you're not prepared at all."

"Have you called Uncle Dave?"

"Yes. He'll be in tonight."

"I'll call Lew. I'll tell him to scratch my name. I did make championship flight, though, Mom. Competition was pretty good, too."

"There's absolutely no reason why you should do that. There's nothing you can do here. Mother wasn't conscious when I called the doctor. She won't know whether you're here or not. No. Go ahead. Grab a sandwich and get back to the course."

"I can't. What if something happens?"

"Nothing is going to happen that quickly. She'd want you to finish what you've begun."

"Don't you want me here with you?"

"Virene is coming. Of course I want you, but I'll need you much more later."

"Okay." I agreed reluctantly. "If you really think so." Mom smoothed back my hair. She managed part of a smile.

"I really think so, Rhys," she said.

The doctor was still with Grandma when I left for the golf course.

I was on the card with Marian again for the championship flight, and I was glad. Part of my mind was back home at Grandma's house. Still I was playing my own game and not paying attention to the competition. So was Marian. I was one shot up on her after the third hole.

"Say," she said as we walked up the fourth tee. "What'd you have for lunch? You've really got your game together this round."

"I guess I just decided losing a golf match isn't fatal. Maybe I'm more relaxed."

"What made you decide that?" Marian asked, planting her tee firmly. Her drive zoomed straight down the fairway, leaving her an easy one-approach lie.

I outdrove her by several yards, but was left with a short approach from the rough. We didn't talk again until we were on the green and waiting for the other two of our foursome to hole out.

"I went home for lunch," I said.

"What?" Marian had forgotten her question, and I wanted to answer it. Not for her, so much, as for myself.

"You asked why I decided this tournament wasn't really important."

"Oh, sure, I remember. So what made up your mind?"

"My grandmother."

"What did she tell you?"

"She didn't tell me anything. She's not well. She's very sick." I walked over to my ball to line up my putt. "She's dying and the doctor was there and I didn't see her. Mom said I should come back here and finish what I'd started." I hadn't felt like crying until I said the words.

Marian glanced at me and walked over to the hole and grabbed the flag.

"Want it in or out?" Her voice was void of expression.

"Out," I answered.

"OK, relax. And take your time."

I sank the fifteen-footer and went two up on Marian.

We were coming up on the seventh hole and I was still holding my two-stroke lead. I was teed up and ready to drive when Marian shouted, "Hold it, Rhys!"

Cutting across the fairway from the clubhouse came Virene, ignoring all the frantic shouts of "Fore!"

"Wyn's asking for you, Rhys," Virene shouted.

I looked at Marian and then at Vi.

"Sure," I said, picking up my ball and tee and slipping my club back into the bag.

"She's winning, you know," Marian said to Vi.

"Wouldn't surprise me," Vi replied, sinking down on the bench and wiping her face with the back of her wrist while I pulled my golf bag from the cart.

Marian came up beside me and placed her hand on my shoulder. "It's not hard to be a winner, Rhys, but it takes class to lose a golf match—or a grandmother."

Virene and I walked back across the course to her car.

I shoved my golf bag in the back seat and climbed in beside Virene. "Is she worse?"

"She's awake. She's been calling for you. And when Wynnie wants anything, I try to get it for her." Vi's big hands were tight on the steering wheel.

We turned out onto the lake road, Virene looking straight ahead, talking to me. "She's one of a kind, Rhys. A grand, grand woman. I've been lucky. All the hours we've spent together over the years."

Somehow I felt very adult and wise, older than Virene. I knew she needed to talk if only to reassure herself that Grandma was still alive.

"I wish I'd known her as well as you do. We weren't together very often."

"Not so much the time, Rhys; it's the things that happen, the things that get shared. Happy and some not so happy." Vi slowed as a car pulled out in front of us.

"Wyn was a beautiful woman. Still is, but when she was younger she was the kind who walked into a room and people stared."

"I know. When we cleaned out the attic, I saw pictures of her."

"It wasn't just her looks. There was something else about her, something that drew people." Vi turned to me. "Whether she intended it or not."

"What do you mean?"

"If you don't know now, you will soon. You're a lot like her. It's a kind of attraction that isn't planned. Half blessing and half curse, Wyn said once."

I'd never had any trouble making friends, but I didn't think that was quite what Vi meant. "What's the curse part?"

"Things can get out of hand before you even know it's happening." Vi was thinking about what she had said. "People start expecting things from you that you haven't promised, and if you're not careful, you find yourself more involved than you intend."

She was making sense. If the summer lasted longer, if Lew and I weren't leaving for different places . . . but Virene was talking about my grandmother! How could I have been so blind!

"You mean a man?" I didn't intend to shout.

"A man," Vi said quietly.

I thought about the letters.

"There was someone besides Grandpa." I didn't bother to make it a question.

Vi's neck reddened. "I didn't say that."

"That's what you meant, wasn't it?"

"Maybe I did. Maybe I didn't." Vi chewed the corner of her mouth.

We rode a few blocks in silence until I asked, "Who was he?"

"It doesn't matter. She stayed with your grandfather

160

and made a good life for both of them. She listened to what her head told her. Now me . . . my heart's always been bigger than my brain."

"Was she right?" I asked.

"Who's to say? She told me once, years later, that if things had been different . . . if the time had been different . . . well. . . . See, she was pregnant with your mother."

The doctor's car was gone when we got home.

18

My Grandmother

"I'll drop you off," Vi said as she pulled up to the curb.

"Aren't you coming in?"

"No." She stared down at her hands. "I'm a coward. I can stand almost anything except good-bye."

Mom was waiting for me when I walked in the house. She hugged me and for a minute I thought she was going to tell me that it had already happened. We looked back out the door. Vi still sat in the car, her head bowed.

"Mother's sleeping. The doctor doesn't think anything is going to happen tonight. Would you mind staying with her while I meet Dave's plane? It gets in at nine. I'm sorry I sent for you, but she woke. She asked for you again."

"It doesn't matter. Golf's just a game. Is she hurting?"

"I don't think so. Most of the time she sleeps."

The doctor came at seven, before Mom left for the airport.

162

"There's nothing we can do for her. Just wait. Her condition is stable. It may be several days."

Mom left. "If the plane's late, I'll call you. Are you sure you will be all right?"

"I'm not afraid, Mother," I said and I wasn't. I hoped it was the same for my grandmother.

When Mom's car pulled out of the drive, I found the classical music station on the kitchen radio, turned it on low, and made my way through the gathering dusk to the porch. I remembered, in the light and shadows, the first night in Grandma's house this summer, and how I had felt, somehow, like a prowler. Now I felt like a keeper.

I sat in the white wicker chair beside the bed and watched the last of the sunlight spill across the lake, copying Grandma's painting.

I reached over and touched the white arm. Her skin was smooth and soft, but I could feel the bone beneath. Although she did not wake or move, there was a nearness between us that I was sure she sensed—some kind of knowing that we shared, which went further than any words we had ever said or could have spoken. The darkness gathered around us, but I did not turn on a light.

I was aware of his presence even though I hadn't heard his footsteps. He hadn't called out my grandmother's name as he usually did. He simply appeared in the doorway, then sat near us on the footstool.

For a while we didn't talk, then he brushed his fingers across my cheek. "You are almost as lovely as Wyn."

I couldn't see his face; the moonlight shone behind, leaving him in darkness.

163

"How did you know?" I asked, sure that he would understand the question.

"Virene called me. She told me that Eve was picking David up at the airport. That you were staying with Wyn. Has she wakened?" He turned away and looked at the moon-streaked lake.

"No."

"Do you mind if I stay? His voice was thick. I sensed, not heard, the tears behind.

I did not answer. I reached out for his hand. His touch was warm and strong and gentle.

"Strange, isn't it? We scream our way into the world and leave it with a sigh. And who's to know which takes more strength."

We stayed like that, linked by touch until Grandma stirred.

"Wid." Grandma's voice was clear. She did not open her eyes.

He stood and moved nearer the bed. "I'm here."

"Of course," she whispered.

She slept again.

He turned and looked out at the lake, his back to me. "The last sip is not the sweetest, Rhys. There must be more. Nothing beautiful happens only once."

I did not answer. There was no need.

Moonlight flooded the lake, lighting the porch. The night was very still.

I closed my eyes and felt their love. I wondered if my mother knew how much had been given up for her . . . if it had been for her.

The three of us were held in a circle of softness, the

164

breeze through the open window barely stirring the sheer curtains, the quiet lap of water against the shore.

Grandma's breathing changed. She began taking deep, deep breaths as if she were sucking in all the air of the world; then came long pauses with no breath at all.

"Rhys?"

"Yes," I said, bending over and taking her hand. Her eyes fluttered open.

"Moon . . . melting."

"I know, Grandma," I whispered.

"Isn't it grand?"

Her eyes closed. Her breathing stopped.

Our Twtti Wyn Hec had flown.